FROM THE SAME AUTHOR

MAGNUS

RISING SUN
TRIUMPHATOR
UNTOLD STORIES

EMPIRE AND THE HAND

W R A I T H

ROBERT ALLEN JOHNSON

Printed in the United States of America

First Printing, November 2015

ISBN: 1515323544

robertallenjohnson.wordpress.com
facebook.com/authorrobertallenjohnson

Cover design by Asher Eggleston
Interior artwork by Jo Gilbert

For Jim and Stacy,
siblings eternal
through thick
and thin.

WRAITH

JD GILBERT 2015

Do not be afraid of the terrors
of the night,
Nor the arrow that flies
in the day.
Do not dread the disease
that stalks in darkness,
Nor the disaster that strikes
at midday.

Psalms 91:5-6

Chapter One

Peace.

Cruel eyes lifted to the heavens in remembrance, to a time when words held truth, not hope. Up and further skyward was his sight drawn; through limbs, leaves, vines, and higher still, where life vanished and only memories remained. *To live there,* he prayed with wordless thought. It was his only wish those dark and dreadful days.

The first drop fell, the second and third not far behind. He cursed the rain, a greater detriment than even wind to his greatest skill in life. *So be it,* he decided and took a silent step forward. *I'll follow deeper.*

The crack of thunder rumbled and passed unnoticed as he prowled stealthily through a maze of grandfatherly roots. The same could not be said for the three men patrolling noisily just a hundred yards distant from the hidden boy. These days, the life of a soldier of the Empire was soft, cushy, and unreasonably comfortable - three descriptions that had never described the young hardened hunter in their midst.

He leaned upon the trunk of a tree, waiting patiently for their nervous laughter to subside, and slowly lifted a leather pouch of water from his left hip to his dry, thirsty lips. The water was cool and pure, revitalizing. He upended the frayed container, poured a small amount into a brown, calloused hand - the hand of a young man who had known nothing but seventeen years of hard work in life. The glistening hand lifted to his face and scrubbed the sweat and dirt from around eyes, nose, and mouth. He blinked away the water; with his free arm, he dried the dampness from an unlined face still smooth and taut with youth.

Both hands reached for his neck to a black mask he lifted to the bridge of a short, wide nose below a pair of black, unflinching eyes. A hood was next, its color a noticeably faded shade of brown, which covered his shoulder-length black hair and darkened his remaining features under the shadow of towering forest trees.

The hunter crouched and crept as close to the

grass-less woodland floor as was possible on two nimble, cat-like legs. Each footfall was perfectly placed and silent; it mattered not that each step was supported by dry leaves and dead limbs, obstacles that forbade the clumsy scouts from wandering too far beyond his sight and hearing. This was his land, his comfort, his territory; he knew each corner, twig, and gully of the forest like an old, familiar friend. His clueless prey did not. All three were unaware they would not escape the day's bloody hunt. They could not.

He took a step; inhaled, exhaled. Took another, did the same. He'd split the distance between himself and the unwelcome intruders in half, could clearly see the deep crimson markings of imperial servitude - three simple lines running up to down, the middle slightly longer - in a field of overlapping black scales on the chest and back of each man. The boy drew nearer and listened as each step landed with a loud metallic clink of scale upon scale, metal upon metal, as the men trudged deeper into thick, humid woodland.

Three against one. The odds didn't concern the boy in the least. He knew the lay of the land better, traveled lighter, could attack from the shadows like a ghost, and vanish like a deadly morning mist. Which of the hapless armor-clad scouts could say the same for themselves? All three were axe-bearers, a foolish weapon of choice for a scout if ever there was one, and none could match his speed or skill with their weighty dual-handed weapons.

The hunter drew his bow, a smooth wooden thing of beauty in its simplicity, and cradled himself in the gnarled roots of a mammoth oak from ancient days of old. There was a dip in the ground here, a gully deep and long enough to hide his brief preparation, and as he hid within its depths, the three soldiers passed from view. From inside of a small dark pouch, he withdrew a string, secured it to the loop on the bottom of the bow, then repeated the process for the top. He reached inside of a sealed waterproof quiver and removed three smooth black arrows, their long heads sharp, unbarbed, and narrow for maximum penetration of armor and flesh. The boy turned each arrowhead down and stuck all three into the soft soil within an arm's reach on his left hand side.

He drew a breath, then pushed himself soundlessly from the trunk of the tree and hug of the roots. From the heights, the sound of rain on leaves filled his ears, a steady drumming that signaled dire weather would be around for hours to come. Nevertheless, the rain mattered not to him. He was dry and content, and so was his weapon.

His head moved slowly, inched itself above the lip of the gully. He studied them, envisioning the fate of each man. The boy cursed them, these *soldiers* who had stolen the peace of his people, of himself. From his knees, he stood to two steady feet, lifted the outstretched bow in clenched right hand, and chose his first target. The string was taut, the fingers of his left hand rough against his masked cheek. One more slow, steady intake of breath, one more blink of darkened eyes. He held his breath.

Deliverance.

The twang of the string filled his ear as the bow reverberated in his hand. The arrow was sure and straight; he kept his eyes on its path as he reached down for the second deadly shaft. He notched the arrow, pulled back on the string once more, glowering as the crimson fountain of blood sprayed from the neck of the first dying soldier. The hunter took aim, let loose, and grabbed for the third and final arrow.

As quickly as that, the first soldier kicked at air and earth in a final bout with death's relentless grip. The second body fell hard upon the forest floor with a cascade of loud metallic clinks, a thud, and a hoarse muffled groan. Two screams filled the drab humid air: one from the second soldier clutching at his chest in a frenzy, the other from the third, yelling, "Where is he?"

The boy pulled his mask down, notched the final arrow, and crossed from darkness into light. "Here!" He held his weapon aloft and saw a pair of wide eyes aghast within the housing of a silver triangular helmet. The string pulled back with ease, its tension an echo of the soldier's fear not twenty yards distant.

"Please, sir!" The panicked voice carried loudly enough for the boy to hear despite being muffled by the full-face imperial helmet. With trembling hand, he tossed the dual-headed axe to the earth with a muted, muffled thud. "You're the one they call *The Ghost?*" The boy's head inclined with pride. He nodded once. "You've won. I surrender. But please, sir...let me bury my friends and return their belongings to their families."

The string drew further back, the bow an easy thing to tame for the hooded youth. The boy spat, taking a silent step forward. "Just as you did for my father? For my friends?"

"Please," the man stammered as he lifted both hands toward the heavens and knelt awkwardly to the ground, "I have never killed a man. I have not even been a scout for two months now. You must understand...I only joined to stay safe...to feed and protect my family!"

"Family?" the youth screamed, the bowstring

drawn further back with the shouted word. "How dare you bring up such a word!"

The soldier raised both hands aloft, removed the helmet, and tossed it noisily to the ground in a show of abject surrender. Terrified eyes lifted to the bowman and he rubbed his tear-stained cheeks with a trembling, balled-up fist. "I'm begging you, kind sir, to only do what's right."

The boy took another step, and then another. "I'm the one with the bow, you coward, and *I* decide what is right! Today, you are condemned and I will leave your accursed body where I so choose: here in the forest for dogs, wolves, and insects to devour and choke upon!" He allowed the soldier a moment's hope, watching as he leapt to his feet to sprint for the safety of the nearest tree. The bowman aimed for the center of the man's back and loosed the final blackened arrow. It lodged itself in the base of the fleeing soldier's neck, severed the spinal cord, and brought the man down like an anchor cast to the depths of a reticent sea.

He waited for the reverberation to fade, let the bow's powerful throb pulsate through his arm and deep into the core of his body before dropping the weapon to his side. With no conscious thought, deft fingers removed the string and returned it to the pouch at his hip. As for the bow, he hoisted it above his head and slid it down his back, its smooth, flexible frame nestled snugly in a brown weathered holster.

Lightning flashed, barely visible beneath the shadow of the leafy green canopy, and the boy withdrew a forearm-length dagger from his belt. *Always approach with caution,* his father had taught him many years ago, a tactic that had saved his life on more than one occasion. Careless and noisy the scouts may have been, but he had witnessed more than one feign death from an arrow strike in the past. Two of the soldiers he knew were dead: the first and the last. The middle one...well, he would find out soon enough.

"Tiro!"

The boy flinched upon hearing his name, fell to the forest floor, and scurried to a nearby tree on hands and knees. He pounded his chest, willing his rapid heartbeat to calm. The soldiers momentarily forgotten in his sudden outburst of fear, he pounded the ground in anger, glancing back at the three bodies behind him. All three sprawled lifelessly across the dark wooded earth, the bloody sight a grotesque scene from a violent nightmare.

"Tiro!" the voice called again, its timbre higher, nearer this time. "I saw you, boy! Come out and help your old man!"

He pushed his head into the dirt, wanted to

scream and release his hate as far into the earth as emotion could carry. Instead, he lifted his head and sheathed the blade still clutched within his tight right fist. "You're not *my old man*, old man!"

"Where are you, boy?" the man called, each step a careless crunch of leaves that warned of each and every move. "I caught some fish and need your help to carry them home. Do you know it's raining?"

Tiro sneered and slid himself across the ground to the base of the tree. Still hidden, he carefully glanced around its edge. The man wasn't even searching for him in the right direction. "Of course I know it's raining! I'm not deaf!"

"Your mother will skin us alive if we don't get home before dinner. Come, boy, help me out."

He envisioned a word from days of old: *justice*. Just another word in a long string of them that failed to even exist anymore. He smirked at the thought of yet another word: a word still very much alive, a word that gnawed at the forefront of his young, bitter mind.

Fate.

The young hunter repeated the familiar steps, a pattern which took no thought and little effort to perform: bow, string, arrow.

He rose from the earth, the hiding place of no import, and took a step toward the man stumbling about with a burden across his old, hunched shoulders. "Stepfather!" he called.

He was off-balance, the pole across his bent shoulders uneven as two buckets full of fish shifted awkwardly with each tentative step. Slowly, carefully he turned toward the cry, stumbled when he saw the deadly weapon aimed straight for his wheezing, heaving chest. "Tiro...! What is this? Enough of your games, child, and help me with-"

"This is not a game, old man!" The boy stepped closer, watching the old man tremble and carelessly drop both buckets of fish to the dense forest floor. "Do you think I'm blind? Do you think my age makes me clueless to my surroundings?"

"Tiro...please! What are you talking about, my boy? Put that thing down or...or point it somewhere else!"

The bowman halted thirty feet from the cowering man who trembled on hands and knees. "I've seen you. I know what you've done."

Wide eyes filled a face of fear. The young boy's stepfather looked around the forest in a daze, raising both quivering hands to his face. "I was-"

"I don't want excuses!" He pulled the arrow to its furthest extent, paused long enough to curse the man a final time, and let hatred propel the arrow forward. It passed clean through the fisherman's neck, who clutched the gaping hole in his throat, a fruitless attempt to staunch the unending geyser of blood. Behind the man, the arrow hummed, the shaft lodging deep within the trunk of a tree. The boy waited, only breathing once the arrow calmed its movement, and the old man fell to his side in an expanding pool of blood.

Tiro stepped forward, first one step and then another, and locked eyes with the man dying on the crimson forest floor. He crouched in front of the face, letting the man writhe a moment more in pain and fear of impending death. He opened his mouth. "I will throw you in the river, old man. No one will ever find you." He swatted aside the hand that reached for him, a final plea for reconciliation, forgiveness, accord. "You will be forgotten. You will die unloved."

The hunter stood, waiting for his stepfather to take his final labored breath before making another move. He lifted his eyes to the heavens, heard the rain, and saw the treetops shift with the ever-changing breeze. The branches swayed, but he felt no gentle brush of air from where he stood and felt no swell of pride or peace within. *It will come,* he assured himself with hollow words as dead as the four men bleeding rivers into wooded earth.

One more job, the boy reminded himself as his hand grasped the hilt of the dagger. He turned to the soldiers, feeling his heartbeat cease within.

Where three had been before, only two remained.

Chapter Two

A full moon hung over a peaceful land. The grass, a vibrant shade of green during the day, reflected moonlight in muted hues of blue and grey. As far as any eye could see, no widespread forest laid claim to the lush flatland between snow-peaked mountains and distant fertile seaside; no pockets of mass familial clusters populated the region aside from those that roamed the plain in packs. Here and there, scattered in what appeared to be random locations across the plain, were nothing more than lonely pillars of bark and limbs, their infrequent placement sporadic at best. So few and far between were they that neither bird nor squirrel made nest within their lofty arms.

Dual lines descended from the northwest, parallel markings pressed deep into the grass, and followed the path of a cart drawn by a man on a horse. The creaking groan of wooden wheels and the occasional hoof on stone were the only sounds one would hear if transported to that sullen, sleepy land.

"There," his voice broke the soft stillness of night. "I told you we were getting close."

If not for the full moon suspended in a black starless heaven, the stream would have gone unnoticed. Then again, it was the fullness of that moon that prompted the late night trek past sundown.

He stroked the brown-black beast along the left side of its neck, waited for his only companion to come to a halt, and leapt to the ground. The grass was thick and untrampled here, its softness reminding him of a cool, feathery pillow. "We'll have a drink and a short rest," the man spoke unashamedly to the animal as both hands unclasped a pair of leather straps connecting the beast to the cart it pulled. "Then we'll follow its course all the way to the shore." He paused to let a smile lift both corners of his dry, parched mouth. "And then it's home. How does that sound?"

The horse whinnied and waited for the man to return from the wagon. It allowed the man to lead it forward through the grass untethered.

With his gloved left hand upon the horse, the man pushed a hood from his head onto a pair of wide, weary shoulders. With his right hand, he adjusted the folds of his cloak, tunic, and riding trousers, all earthy shades of browns and greys reflecting silver in the moonlight. The last time he'd bothered to check, his rough black beard had shown surprising signs of premature silver as well.

His eyes were drawn to the sphere in the sky, its brightness more than adequate for the current nighttime journey. "Just another hour or so," he spoke as his hand moved from the horse's flank to the reins upon its neck. Looking around the field, he left the thin leather straps where they dangled and returned his hand where it previously rested. "There is too much light tonight to go unused."

He was drawn to the stream; to its sparkle, to its sound. The beast was as well, and the traveler trusted his four-legged companion enough to let it walk unrestrained to its edge. The grass began to thin. In its place, a gently sloping bed of dirt peppered with countless rounded stones and tiny white pebbles. The man paused, considering the long, watery journey each stone had undergone in ages past to reach the very bank he stood upon.

Kneeling at the stream's edge, he removed his gloves and set both in the dirt beside him. He pushed his loose sleeves just above his elbows – first his right, then his left – and reached outward with both palms toward the moon.

The water was swift and cold. He cupped his hands beneath the flow, lifting them to his mouth; once more, they descended into the stream and back again to his mouth. "Wonderful, isn't it?" he asked the beast, its front legs no impediment to the water rushing around them, its head pointed downward in the free-flowing stream. "But let's not get too lazy, now. We still have many miles to go yet."

He lifted his hands once more from the stream and raised them to his head, feeling the coldness revitalize him as it dripped across his clean-shaven head, and watched the rivulets run into and out of his thick, unkempt beard. His hand rubbed at closed eyes, their wide almond shapes a foreign sight in the land he trudged through. When they opened, they fell upon the reflection staring back at him. When was the last time he'd dared to look? His left hand rubbed the remaining droplets from a beard as silver as it was black. Just as quickly as the shock had come, it fell forgotten in the stream. *Have you really grown so old?* he asked himself, the lines across his forehead and around those deep brown eyes drawing his attention from the silver beard.

A splash to his left startled him from a silent detour through paths of vanity. "What is it?" he asked his voiceless companion in a whisper much too loud for comfort. He saw the long head bob up and down momentarily, noticing the two animal ears unlike his own twitch as the horse backed itself away from the stream. With left hand outstretched, the man stepped slowly toward the nervous animal. "Peace now. Here is my hand." He grabbed the reins, lifted them over the quivering ears and head, and wrapped them around his wrist. "What did you hear? A snake? A fox?" He dismissed each question as nonsense as soon as it was spoken. The beast was rarely spooked, and never by anything less than wolf or bear.

He reversed course alongside the now skittish animal and felt the ground rise with each step, sensing the cushion of grass return underfoot. He chanced a glance away from the stream and saw the cart between the horse and himself at a distance of twenty paces or more. There was a sword there. "Fool," he cursed himself, knowing full well he had removed the weapon from the horse's flank mere hours ago. He removed some slack from the reins, took another step backward to match the slow retreat of his companion, and crouched low enough to reach the knife inside of his right knee-high boot. A cascade of breadcrumbs trickled back into his boot, a messy result from a rushed mid-evening stop for dinner.

"Steady yourself, Yuzy," the man spoke aloud

as the nervous animal stumbled in its rearward retreat. "Stay with me now. Do you hear me?" The horse jerked its head sharply upward, the reins and its master's wrist following right behind. "No running. No bolting." He pointed the knife toward the wagon, its current location a distant diagonal beyond the horse's head and the stream. "We need to get there - to the cart. Forward now, boy."

The beast struggled against his attempt at forward motion, pulling its head again skyward. "Don't do this to me, Yuzy. Not here! Not now!" Another jerk freed the reins from his hands. He felt the reins brush against his fingertips, grasped at the emptiness of air, and winced as momentum brought him painfully into the grass on hands and knees. The man watched the animal gallop full speed across the blue-grey field, saw it shrink in size until it disappeared at last from sight and sound. He wondered how far the beast would run for safe respite.

An unsettling shift in the air drew his attention back to the other predicament at hand. Still on his knees and unable to see down the bank into the stream, he cocked his head and tried to place what might have disrupted the beast from its unplanned nighttime drink. Staying as close to the earth as was possible, he set his sights upon the cart once more. The hilt of the sword called to him, its leather-wrapped handle propped neatly against the side of the two-wheeled wagon. He could see traces of silver glimmer between its webbing, the polished metal around the scabbard reflecting moonlight.

A splash broke the unnatural silence. Then another, louder and closer than the first, followed by a series of stones racing downhill in a frantic rush for water. As the landslide came to an abrupt, noisy halt, the stillness of deserted midnight was drowned by a wail of despair and a harsh, inhuman hiss. The man clutched the knife in his hand, sank further into the thick grass, and prayed for concealment. Three more cracks filled his ears, the sound of splitting stone and earth, of ancient roots carelessly torn asunder. He pushed himself upright and let his feet carry him to the cart and the only object that could slow his swelling fear. He reached for it, letting the comforting sound of metal gliding across wood fill the air as the two-handed weapon left the safety of its scabbard. He returned the knife to his boot.

Armed and upright, he turned to face the stream and the threat that left him horseless and abandoned in the night. To his left, the water flowed freely; before him, the earth had been disrupted, a collection of stones and earth jutting cruelly into the path of the southbound tributary.

The flow of water was impeded but not halted, a dam left conspicuously incomplete. No beast could work with such speed, skill, or precision, so his eyes darted up and down the bank for the outline of human form. He saw nor heard one, turned his face north past the dammed stream and back again to the hillside beyond the stream. From beyond its crest appeared a darkened being, a light-less emptiness cloaked in shadow.

The man clutched the sword, raising it defensively before himself. "Who's there? What do you want?" His query went unanswered. "I'm just a traveler stopping for a drink and will then be on my way."

The emptiness moved to the edge of the hill and extended an inky tendril from within itself. The traveler, immobile, watched aghast in disbelief as it snaked its way through the air toward him. The moon cast no light upon it and a bitter cold preceded its path down the hill, across the stream, and up the embankment toward the quivering man. "Arach," it spoke with the same inhuman hiss as before. "Come."

He struck out at the tendril, losing his balance as the sword passed harmlessly through the mass-less apparition. As he righted himself and lifted the sword in conscious fear, Arach saw the blade frost over and turn a cold shade of pale blue. The tendril lifted itself beyond slashing distance and poised midair as if to strike. "How do you know me? Who told you my name?"

The being remained silent and moved further down the hill toward the half-dammed stream.

"Please leave me be," he called as his eyes moved from the hovering tendril to the shapeless darkness before him. "I have nothing of value!"

A trilling hiss resonated across the stream, a mockery of laughter that prompted the armed traveler to take a step back, and then another. "That is not for you to decide, man." With a voiceless command, the tendril struck much like the stinger of a scorpion, passed through the useless sword, and came just short of Arach's unprotected throat. Frost consumed the blade once more, and the worthless weapon splintered and fell in a hundred icy fragments at the traveler's feet. "Come with me."

Wide eyes upon the shadow, Arach knelt and grabbed the knife within his boot. Still kneeling, he threw the dagger for its center, watching it sail through the shadow and into the dirt behind. He heard its sharp metallic quiver, heard its blade shatter, and saw its pieces trickle gently down the hillside toward the edge of the stream. He stayed on his knees, feeling the helplessness drag his arms and head to the earth beneath him. "Kill me or leave me be!" he managed despite his fear. "I'm not here to cause you any harm. I swear it's so! I'm just a lonely man passing through - no more, no less!"

"Lonely?" it hissed, its ghastly arm detracting from the cowering traveler. "Do you know what it is to be lonely, Arach?"

"You know my name, wraith." He clutched at the grass, forcing his eyes to rise to his inquisitor. He could see no face, no solid shape, no mass, nor weight. "You must also know my answer."

The frigid trill sounded once again as the darkness reversed its path from the foot of the hill, beginning a slow ascent up the grassy hill. "Perhaps you are lonely, man...but not as lonely as the dead you've left behind."

The traveler's face lifted in defiance, burning volcanic with anger. "Why are you here, wraith? Say what you will and be gone."

"I have plenty more to say, human." It crested the hill, its inhuman form floating inches above the grass beneath. "Are you ready to listen? If so, then follow me."

The darkness departed, and with it, the unruly cold. Arach rose from his knees, looked around, and opened his ears to the night. The soothing lullaby of water over stone filled his ears, blocking out all else. He edged closer to the stream, scanned its bank for the gloves he'd left behind, and saw them floating downstream one right after the other. He didn't bother reclaiming them, didn't consider taking a drink at the water's edge. Instead, he splashed his face and willed himself to stay awake.

His eyes began to droop, exhaustion finally taking root, and he grabbed a shard of the fragmented sword. The sting of its edge a welcome boon between his trembling, calloused fingers, the man lifted it to his eyes, studied its jagged edge, and flicked the useless sliver away. "Stay awake," he spoke aloud and chanted the simple words thrice more before his aching body succumbed to exhaustion at long last.

Chapter Three

"What is it?"

Softly, Tiro closed the door and leaned against its unsturdy wooden frame. His hand fell, touching the rough-hewn wall of crudely painted planks. He remembered those days - hazy, distant days - when each pointed nail was lifted to the hand of a smiling, loving father. Eight years past - half a lifetime for the breathless, anxious hunter - the small house of wood and bamboo went up piece by foraged piece. Today, if the boy paused long enough to listen, each wall, door, cabinet, and table whispered tales of older, better days; days when father and son had time enough to build, time enough to simply live. *Two more, Father,* he thought, and forbade his weary mind and body from collapsing in upon him. *And one who tried to take your place.* "Nothing."

The girl stared daggers through the male image of herself. "Tiro!" she snapped, the sudden noise drawing him out of a near-stupor, and tossed the afternoon's chore - a basket full of half-peeled potatoes - onto a rickety countertop. "Look at me!"

He watched his twin approach and pushed himself from the closed door, ignoring her unblinking, probing eyes. She could read his inner thoughts as well as he could hers, and direct eye contact only magnified the bothersome ability tenfold. Instinctively, reflexively, he changed the dangerous subject. "Potatoes again, then?"

She conceded Round One and moved on to the next. "Potatoes go well with meat, which is what I assumed you'd be bringing back from your hunt."

"I got sidetracked." Tiro dug into his pocket, removing two square imperial shoulder insignias. "Caught them unaware."

His sister fingered the roughly cut cloth and studied the familiar crimson markings on each one. "Were they officers?"

He shook his head and untied the quiver at his left hip, proceeding to remove each layer of hunting gear one piece at a time. "Scouts. New sheep among the fold, by the looks of them."

"How much do you think you'll get for these?"

Tiro smirked, well pleased with his twin's burgeoning business sense. He studied her contemplative, prudent face, sensing the girl tug at invisible monetary levers within her quick adolescent mind. "The Hand always pays well. I suppose it's the cost of being rebellious." Examination complete, he reached a hand out for the insignias he would exchange for cash. "My guess is half a month's supply of food and grain for each."

The dark-haired girl returned to the counter, reclaimed her knife, and lifted an unpeeled vegetable from the half-filled basket. "That's good news, Tiro. I see plenty of potatoes in our future."

The hunter removed the sheathed bow from his back, playfully nudging her with it as he left the girl to finish her mid-afternoon work. "If you buy so much as one potato with that money, I swear I'm going to tell Marik you snore so loud the walls can't help but move."

Delicate face and neck turning a noticeable shade of red, she smirked and threw a handful of potato skins at the rapidly closing door. "You're evil, brother!"

The words, tossed thoughtlessly in jest at his quickly retreating back, brought the boy to a sudden standstill. He swallowed the uncomfortable lump in his throat, wishing the joy within her heart could somehow fill his own.

*

The twins sat across from each other at a square wooden table, a lonely bowl of steaming red potatoes placed perfectly in its center. A trio of wooden plates sat vacant before three wooden table stools, three untouched pairs of eating utensils on the right hand side of each plate. In the empty space - his mother's seat - a folded, tattered cloth claimed the spot of the missing plate. Tiro watched a steaming trail of heat rise to the ceiling and vanish into nothingness. The girl looked down, unreadable eyes downcast, raven hair pulled back in a simple waist-length ponytail, and toyed with the hem of her fur-lined maroon blouse.

"I don't understand. Are you sure you didn't see him?" his mother asked from the open doorway, her small, fragile frame and slightly hunched back toward the two seated children. The dark, seemingly impenetrable wall of towering forest trees to the east held her focus, their thickness, depth, and height a mockery refusing her a moment's peace. "He was no more than an hour behind you, Tiro."

"I already told you, Mother," he answered, each word laced with more than a touch of annoyance, "I was preoccupied with more important things."

"But you must have seen him?"

"Why do you even care so much?" The boy pushed himself from table's edge, the tri-legged stool toppling to the smooth wooden floor with a crash and a clatter. "I hate that man."

"Tiro!" she exclaimed in horror, a quick look of disgust passing over her countenance as she looked her only son up and down. "*That man* is your stepfather - my husband - and he deserves your respect!"

He paced the short length of room that passed as a kitchen and dining area, then stabbed at a steaming potato with his knife. "Tara hates him too," he added, lifting the potato to his mouth. He blew the steam, watching its smoky path glide parallel to the floor before rising to vanish from sight, and ignored the ferocious glare from his silent twin sister.

The matron of the house shifted her attention from the brazen young boy to the only one still seated. "Tara? What's your brother talking about? Is this true?"

The hem of her blouse was inviting once more, and the girl's gaze averted self-consciously from her mother's bewildered stare. Tiro swallowed the potato whole, turning his attention back toward his only sister. He swallowed and ran an arm across his face. Above the arm, he studied her - saw the quiver of fidgeting hands beneath the table, the unconscious tremor of her entire right leg. Hatred and frustration spiking once more, he took a step toward his mother. "Of course it's true!" He tossed the knife upon the table and resumed his repetitious journey across the room once more.

"You children are terrible," the woman tutted and returned her fearful gaze eastward. "Do you expect him to be perfect? Well, he's not! No man is." She offered a cutting sidelong glare at the rapidly pacing boy who simply ignored the look. "If you're so wise, then tell me: what should I have done after your father's passing? Sit around and cry? Do you think a woman's tears make for good soup? Well?" She stared arrows into the still-pacing boy, daring him to stop and face her. "I did my best for you." She pointed at the twins, first one and then the other. "All for you. What was I supposed to do? Sit around and let us all starve to death?"

In a rage, Tiro spun on his heel, pointed an outstretched trembling finger at his sister, and faced the woman who bore the pair in pain seventeen long years before. "A life of slow starvation would have been better than-"

"Tiro!" his sister yelled as she lifted a clenched red fist from her lap and pounded hard upon the table. Tears filled her eyes, pouring silent rivers down smooth brown cheeks. Flooded eyes glistening, the wordless stare begged caution, discretion. "Enough," she whispered, her soul pleading desperation with that of her twin's. "Enough!"

Tension thick, a harsh whisper was all their mother could muster. "What's going on? Better than what?"

The hunter reached for his knife, wiped the potato-covered blade on his pants leg, and pushed past his mother toward the open door. "Reality, Mother. Better than reality."

Hands upon her hips, she let her son be. "If you're going to throw a tantrum and leave, boy, perhaps you should try to make yourself useful and find your stepfather. At least he has the smarts to be out looking for food when someone else does not."

Tiro stormed from the house, making for the only shelter he claimed. The hunter knew his mother well, knew she'd be watching and mocking each swift, hurried step from the open doorway to his rear. Fuming, he pierced the forest depths, pounded a gloveless fist into his thigh, and plunged deep enough to be well hidden from all threat of prying, chasing eyes.

He stopped, breathed purity and life into young, constricted lungs. Bark-covered pillars rose majestically from a cold flat ground of dry, dead leaves, connecting themselves to massive clouds of green in lofty heights. The forest bore no doorway, no window, no wall, or even room, but safety and solace knew no equal there. He found a large familiar tree and sat with a grunt, his back firm against the thick grey bark.

The crackle of dry leaves turned his head.

"I know that pout." A tall, slender boy appeared from forest's edge, his family's house the nearest building to the thick line of trees. He kicked the ground with each step, smiled, and placed both weaponless hands behind his long, muscular back. The black-haired boy walked straight for Tiro's tree and took a seat at the hunter's right hand. Even seated, he was a good half a head taller than the bowman on his left. "Want to talk?"

Tiro shook his head. "Not tonight, Marik." His hand reached into his pocket, removing the two red insignias. "But look what the ghost dragged in this afternoon."

The tall boy whistled, impressed, and held out a hand to see for himself. He turned them in his hands, observing the simple design of three crimson brushstrokes. "You always amaze me, my friend. So when will you take them in and claim your bounty?"

"Tomorrow or the day after. I'll need to send a message first, find out where they're hiding." He accepted the colorful patches back from his friend. "Want to go with me this time? Meet some new people?"

The boy's head shook and he stretched his long legs, laying both flat upon the ground. "Too much work to do."

"Around the house? Or with Tara?"

Marik chuckled and elbowed his sulking friend. "Tara is never work. You know that."

"She's a good girl." Tiro fingered a stick, flicking it as far from himself as was possible. Deep in thought, he nodded to himself. "As soon as you're ready, Rik, you have my blessing." A palatable silence hung between them, but he continued on regardless. "I want her out of the house. I'd have packed her bags and led her to your doorstep years ago, my friend." He felt the boy's eyes upon him and shifted nervously under their weight. "If only the days hadn't been so dark and uncertain."

"Years ago?" the boy asked, a sad smirk clinging to his upper lip as he tried to change the mood of conversation for the better. He knew that life had been a long, brutal journey for the boy beside him and had never understood the hellish depths his path had plunged. Nevertheless, fear had kept Marik silent, an unease which stilled his frozen tongue, and year after year had passed with nothing more than mysterious silence between the two friends. He assumed it would be as such for years and years to come. "Wouldn't that have been a sight? A couple of twelve-year-old newlyweds running rings around the mainland..." He left the thought unfinished.

Tiro sighed and leaned forward, wrapping both arms around his raised right knee. "Ah, but that would have been better. Safer."

"Eighteen is just around the corner," added Marik, the sadness from his friend's sour mood fading into brighter shades of excitement. A grin returned to the bright eyes lifted high. "Tara and I promised my folks to wait until then. I'm sure we can wait another month, so long as you can."

Reticent, the friends stared forward, beholding the familiar routine of a village settling into peaceful twilit slumber. Women hoisted lanterns into place on small wooden porches, doorways sealed shut to the impending nightfall, and dozens of windows transformed into thin shining frames, the dim glow and flicker of candles within creating the illusion of priceless golden etchings.

"But what about you, Tiro? What will you do?" the boy asked with eyes set forward. He swallowed, surprised that his bravery had finally bested his timidity. It was a question he'd been wanting to ask for months now. "I mean, when

Tara finally leaves home?"

The hunter sighed, lifting the dual imperial insignias from the afternoon's kill to eye-level. "The pursuit of happiness."

Marik crossed his arms. The answer, although unsurprising, released a wave of sorrow in his chest. "We need you here, Tiro. All of us do; and not just your own family."

"So does The Hand."

The tall boy tensed, gritting his teeth audibly. "To the rebels, you're just another efficient killer with a bow they didn't pay for. Don't they have enough of those?"

"Not nearly enough. So long as the Empire continues to grow, so should The Hand." He paused, sensing the disconnect within his friend, intentional or not. "The Empire is growing, Marik. Growing in number and in boldness; forcing their way of life on us and all who stand in their way. Isn't it our duty to stop them? To protect ourselves, our families, our land?"

"Sometimes," Marik began before halting mid-thought. The Empire and The Hand were touchy subjects with the young hunter. Caution and tact were his greatest allies when scaling dangerous territory such as this. "Sometimes, I wonder if it would be best to just capitulate." The young bowman's head darted sideways, incredulity painted across his face. "For once, just hear me out, Tiro. I want a family, a peaceful life. A wife and children. That's what I long for most in life - you know this." He pulled his knees to his chest, scratched at his nose. "So if peace can be granted with the bend of a knee and a small monthly fee, how could I not pause to consider those simple, basic terms?"

Tiro wanted to scream, to pound some sense into the nonsensical, clueless boy. How many times had he and Marik had this same, repetitive discussion on right versus wrong, imperialism versus independence? He had lost count years ago. "You know it's so much more than that, Rik. Besides," he added with the shake of his head to rid himself of a blossoming poisonous irritation toward his friend, "it's the Empire who should be bowing to us - to the people - and not the other way around."

Marik grabbed his friend at the nape of his neck and gave it a calm, loving squeeze - a simple, useful tactic to bring the easily exasperated boy back to earth from his lofty pedestal of strong, indefatigable belief. "Perhaps you're right. What do I know? I only wish we could all get along without so much hatred and bloodshed."

Tiro shrugged. Those particular side effects didn't bother him much, if at all.

In the distance, a dim lantern bobbed and dipped from left to right as if held by a wandering ghost. The boys watched in silence, staring as it wound itself from a ramshackle guard post at the corner of town to a winding dirt path. From the path, it crossed a narrow wooden walkway, hurried along one of many branches of the platform that stemmed in each and every direction through the quiet, sleepy village. Straight through a clearing between houses it snaked before disappearing behind a hut one instant, reappearing on its other side a moment later. Tiro watched with growing unease, feeling a stone in his stomach materialize, enlarge, and sink deeper with each twist and turn of the floating lantern's path until, at last, the ghastly bearer found its final destination. The evening air was warm, no breeze alive to penetrate the dense forest encircling the boys. Still, Tiro began to shiver.

The hurried, frantic knock reached their ears from where they sat, the creak of an opening door shortly thereafter. Tiro held his breath and hardened his heart, waiting for the sound he knew was sure to come.

"What's that—?" Marik asked, the heartbreaking wail of his best friend's mother cutting his query short. He jumped to his feet with a start, reached down for his friend, who was still seated in a wordless daze. "Something's wrong, Tiro! We need to go!"

He allowed the hand to lift him and felt its strength envelop his weakness. He was sinking, drowning, the suddenly frigid night threatening to overwhelm him. He didn't expect this, didn't expect it to happen so soon. Tiro shut his ears to the screams within his head, following his friend through the towering line of trees, into the clearing, and past a cluster of poorly constructed houses. He stumbled, letting the haunted glow of lantern light and the heart-wrenching sob of death-discovered lead his heavy footsteps home.

Chapter Four

Arach heard a thud and opened his eyes to a cloudless, sapphire sky. *Blessed light,* he thought before cursing himself for falling asleep through the night. He was cold and clammy; he lifted his aching head, rubbing the pain and dirt from behind his ears. He let his eyes fall to his feet and saw both resting in the current of the free-flowing stream.

The thud sounded again from behind the slope; near enough to cause concern but just beyond his line of sight. *Bandits,* he guessed with a silent wince. *They must have found the cart.*

The traveler rolled from his back to his belly as quietly as he could, feeling the water slosh around his feet within the boots. *Of all the places to find trouble,* he continued to himself with a humorless grin and left the unfortunate thought unfinished.

Controlled by years of thoughtless instinct, his right hand reached inside the soggy boot for the forearm-length dagger and found nothing but wet, silt-covered leather. There was no time to remove the cumbersome boots, which was well enough with him. As soon as he'd have time to remove the soaking footwear, they would surely take hours to dry.

He pulled himself forward across the dirt and pebbles by his elbows and knees, looked left and right for a weapon sufficient for his own defense. The largest stone in sight was a misshapen white oval the size of his thumb, which wouldn't do at all. Another half-minute of crawling through the dirt brought him side-by-side with a handful of metallic shards from the night before. Although the sun had risen high enough to expel any trace of morning cold, the memory of the midnight confrontation forced Arach to bury his face into the earth as a wave of uncontrollable shivers subsided.

Another thud preceded a dull cascade of soft objects falling one atop the other, followed by an all-too-familiar inhuman noise. The man raised his head from the dirt, the sound beyond the grassy crest more captivating than the magical refrains of a carnival bard. He whistled musically and heard his companion neigh in response. "Yuzy!" he cried as he pushed himself up from the pebble-lined bank. "Did it never cross your mind to wake me first?"

The horse looked his way and stomped the ground impatiently. Scattered around the grass to the rear of the cart were dozens of apples. An empty burlap sack hung half in, half out the wooden cart. "Never in my life has man nor beast seen grass as lush and green as this," Arach said with the wave of a hand and unmasked joy in his voice, "but still you choose dessert before breakfast." Arms outstretched, he covered the remaining distance between himself and the horse in a few quick strides, allowing the beast to nuzzle his chest as both arms wrapped tightly around the neck. "You proved wiser than me last night, old boy. Maybe I should follow your lead more often."

He unclasped his arms, bent over, and grabbed an apple from the grassy pile. Lifting the fruit to his mouth, he leaned against the wooden cart and savored the first juicy bite. "No sword, no knife," he paused as he craned his head to glimpse the stream sparkling in the morning sun, "and not a clue." He held the unfinished apple to the horse, who ignored it in favor of an unchewed one from the pile. Arach took another bite of the red fruit and set it on the cart beside him. "But at least we have food. And the stream will provide our water. I suppose those are the two most important things for now."

Under the watchful gaze of his four-legged companion, Arach struggled mightily with his left, then right boot. More than a trifle winded, he pinpointed the location of the sun and placed the two knee-high boots right side up in the back of the cart. "You and I have a bit of exploring to do, Yuzy," he said and brushed both hands against his dirt-covered sides. "But I'd rather go barefoot for now than squish my way noisily across the grass."

He eased himself from cart-side and knelt in the grass with a painful groan. His back hurt like fire. A night spent upon dirt and stones would do that to any man even half his age. He reached for the loose collection of apples. "Don't get me wrong: I'm more than thrilled that you found your way back. But it would be a reward beyond all measure," he dropped a handful of the round red fruit into the rough brown sack, "if I actually had a companion who cleaned up after himself every once in a while."

The last apple in its place, he stood to his bare feet with a pleasant crack in his back. "A man can wish, can't he?" He stepped toward the embankment, felt the lush grass envelop his dirty, calloused feet. North to south, his eyes scanned the length of stream before him. His focus turned upon the adjacent, unexplored hill just east of the stream bed and whatever lie beyond. "I need your nose, Yuzy. Come with me."

Head upright and ears rotating ever so slightly, the beast approached its master without protest. At the edge of the embankment where the grass began to thin, Arach grasped the small leather pommel and lifted himself into the saddle with ease. He adjusted the twisted reins from his companion's nighttime run and stroked the black hair running up and down its long neck. "No more running, all right? At least, not without me."

He nudged the horse and leaned away from the descent, allowed a moment's rest for the animal to drink its fill of water. Arach scanned the hill, saw nothing; watched the upright ears hovering above the stream, knew the beast was vigilant despite its brief respite. "Up we go, boy," he ordered with a gentle push of bootless ankles.

Horse and rider moved into the flow of water barely reaching the curve of the animal's underside. Arach stretched his feet and skimmed its surface, feeling the current rush above, below, and all around his skin. His thoughts turned to its source, to a faraway mountain bearing snowy shoulders stretched toward the heavens. Its icy peaks brought life and fertility to the distant shore and all lands in between. He had been to that place once before as a young man, had sipped the infant drops of newborn springtime.

Man and beast came up from the water, shaking the clinging droplets from feet and fur. The ground began to rise and, with it, Arach as well. Standing tall in the stirrups, he lifted his head, straining to catch a glimpse of unseen land beyond the eastern rise. He brought a hand to his brow, squinted through the sunlight, and returned to the saddle once the beast had crested the hill to find flat ground.

"What do you see?" Arach asked his mute companion. "Anything out of the ordinary?" He looked left and right, unsure what he was looking for; smelled the air, and realized his sense of smell was nothing compared to that of the creature beneath him. He looked back upon the embankment, envisioning the previous night's encounter. The shattered fragments of useless weapons mocked him as he visualized the moonlit retreat of the lightless being. "This way," he said with a southward pull of the reins before adjusting their course for a more southeasterly route.

"What sane man-?" Arach began under his breath before cutting himself short. He stood upright in the stirrups once again, denying the blossoming sense of disquiet anything more than a crumbling foothold. "There," he pointed, "and there. And another behind the stone. They're everywhere."

Horse and rider glided gently across the thick blanket of grass, passed between a morbid string of animals frozen in life's last horrid moment before an unforeseen death. Satisfied that he and Yuzy were indeed alone, Arach leapt to the earth with the reins wrapped tightly around his left wrist. He approached the first dead badger of five in sight, leaning in toward its dark, furry face. Its eyes were wide, staring straight through the traveler, and its small, harmless mouth open mid-shriek. He grabbed a lonely stone from nearby, nudged the foot-long mammal's belly, and rolled the stiff animal onto its back. Arach recoiled at the sight of an oily black substance pouring slowly from the animal's cold, lifeless heart.

He dropped the stone from a hand now quivering with uncontrollable trepidation, took a step closer to his companion, and mounted the fidgety beast. His eyes never left the thick blackness oozing from the stiff, dead badger. "Perhaps it's time to leave this place, Yuzy." The horse needed no further prodding as it turned in its place toward the stream not far behind.

The being struck without warning, its tendril a lightning strike from the churning, smoky darkness deep within itself. The horse collapsed, Arach following close behind in a sharp, downward plummet. He rolled in the grass, righted himself, and knelt on hands and knees ten feet from the edge of the hill. The sun was behind him, its beams swallowed whole by the partially translucent wraith hovering on the edge of the hillside. He saw the beast kick at the earth, watched as a clod of grass-covered dirt flew through the air to land beside the stream.

"You've seen my collection," the darkness spoke, an apparent note of glee clinging to each hissed word. It recoiled the tendril still lodged within the horse and pulled it slowly toward itself where it vanished inside of the shapeless darkness. A prairie dog lay prone in the dirt before the ever-shifting being. "Come. Eat. This is my gift to you, Arach."

The traveler steadied himself as a wave of nausea threatened to overcome him. "Who are you?"

"Eat first," it commanded.

Arach watched the darkness twist, boil, and bubble from within itself, held back a painful acidic retch, and cleared his throat. "I would rather drink in peace and be on my way. I have a long journey ahead of me. Just let me pass, wraith."

"There is life inside this animal yet," it hissed with a swirling motion toward the prairie dog. "Even in death, Arach. Come; see for yourself.

Drink of its blood. It will satisfy you more than the stream ever could. Or do you wish to be thirsty again as soon as your hand departs your lips?"

He pulled himself to his feet, looking at the thick, oily blackness seeping from the animal in the grass. "You killed my horse. I don't trust you." One step was all he needed. The first led to the second, and the third and fourth led to more. "I'm going home, wraith. And because of you, I must now walk."

The emptiness grew, blackened, and shrieked from a wide-open cavernous mouth. Arach raised his arms to his head, closed his eyes, and tried to shut his ears to the sound. When he opened his eyes, the being was gone. The prairie dog remained where it was, covered in a grotesque pool of the thick black substance.

From behind, a noise pierced the sudden stillness. "Yuzy!" he cried as the beast lifted groggy head and stood to four unsteady legs. The scene reminded Arach of the first steps his companion had taken shortly after its birth not six years earlier. "This time, we must truly leave. And quickly."

With a hand on the horse's neck, the traveler helped the unsteady beast down the hill, through the stream, up the adjacent slope, and back to the abandoned cart. He removed his dripping cloak, changed into an old but dry pair of trousers, and tossed the wet clothes beside his still-drying boots. With no time to spare, he reattached the cart to the now steady-footed horse, grabbed a pair of apples, and left the accursed place far behind.

Chapter Five

"I can do this for you, you know."

Tara glanced sidelong at her twin, each short muffled step she took a mirror image of his own. "No you can't, Tiro. It's a woman's job." Her voice was hushed, strained. The two walked side by side on a slightly elevated path of planks, their purposeful height and placement unneeded in the later months of dry, green summers. Each rainy spring, however, the wooden spider web of pathways provided a necessary means of transport between buildings in the small, forest-hugging village. "Are you a woman?"

"I'm your brother." The two reached their destination, a wide and low rectangular hut in the center of the village, its size a noticeable eight times larger than a standard home within the town. Tiro turned and faced his sister, placing both hands upon his hips. He blocked the only doorway leading in and out of the quiet building, noticing she had mimicked his own posture. His hands dropped to his side. "I would do anything for you. No one has to know."

"I know you would, Tiro." She let her own guard down and clutched a bundle of folded clothing to her chest. Eyes upon the closed door behind her brother, she took a breath, expelling it audibly. "But I need to do this. For myself." Her attention shifted from the door to his chin. "To know for sure."

"He is dead, sister."

Something in his voice - something hidden or purposely veiled - prompted Tara to lift her eyes to his. Tiro dropped his gaze, self-conscious and guilt-ridden. "Come inside. Wait for me, brother."

He paused in thought, nodded in admiration of her courage and grit. Tiro took a hesitant step back, opened the door inward for his waiting sister.

A long, narrow waiting room greeted the twins as they crossed the threshold. The interior of the building included a host of doors on a wall facing the entryway, many of which opened to small rooms of treatment. Other rooms housed nothing more than low-lying tables and spices needed to prepare the dead for burial. Tara's sight fell upon the one closed door in a long line of them.

"Good morning, Tiro, Tara," a voice called from the far side of the low-lit waiting room. The middle-aged man wore a long blue robe full of pockets and stood up from behind a long cluttered desk. His back was to a pair of tall book-filled shelves, half of their contents seemingly strewn across the desk itself. He placed a circular-looking glass upon a pile of open books and crossed the long empty room with a slow, easy gait. "Please accept my condolences for your stepfather." He bowed his head and lifted an outstretched hand, a simple gesture for the girl to follow. "His body arrived during the night. A fisherman from Sver found him floating downstream. One of the other villagers recognized him and sent a messenger to find your mother. Anyway," he stopped beside the closed door, placed his hands behind his back, "I'm sure you spoke with him last night."

"Mother did, yes," Tara answered, emotion a lifeless corpse within her.

The doctor paused, considered his words. "Your father was in worse shape. Diyavl here is battered and bruised but still in one piece." He looked from one twin to the other. "I haven't had time to remove his clothes or clean him. Your mother said I should expect you."

"Thank you, doctor," she managed in reply as she stepped past the man, pushed the door open without another word, and removed herself from sight. A soft clink of metal upon metal filled the room, and the lock on the far side of the door slid firmly in place.

The hunter sensed the doctor's prying eyes on him and squirmed under the unwanted visual contact. "Tiro...forgive the intrusion, but I can't help but wonder how a man as fit as your stepfather found himself alone and washed down river. Unless I'm mistaken, he spent most of his life on or along the water. Am I mistaken?"

Tiro shifted uncomfortably, glancing around the narrow room. Unsure what to do with himself, he made for a lonely stool against the wall, brushed its surface off, and sat down heavily. "I didn't know the man when he was a child, so I don't think I can answer that." He looked up and saw the doctor's perturbation visibly spark. "My stepfather was a drunk. Don't tell me you didn't know that."

Unhappy with the sudden cross-examination, the blue-robed doctor crossed his arms. "I did. In fact, we spoke about it a time or two if you could believe as much."

The boy leaned forward, studying a passing shadow beneath the closed door. "Then it looks like we've solved your mystery."

"Perhaps." The doctor paused, waiting for Tiro to continue or show a hint of remorse. The boy sat stock still, dark eyes glued to the door where sister and stepfather remained. "Well...if that is all."

Apparently, it was. Eyelids turning heavy, the hunter succumbed to boredom and cast the world into pitch-black darkness. Half an hour later, he jerked himself awake as the gentle scraping sound of the security latch woke him from haunted dream state. He raised his blurry eyes and saw the door yawn to reveal the feminine outline of his sister. She held a drab old bag - their stepfather's clothes, Tiro assumed - and shuffled her way out of the small room, into the waiting area. While her attention fixed solely on the door, Tiro stood to his feet and pulled it open with a creak.

"Good day, children," the doctor called, his voice hushed and distant from behind the pile of books. Tara nodded, her appreciation clearly forced, and Tiro followed suit.

He followed her out the door, breathing deeply of the clean fresh air. Behind him, the door slammed in place; before him, his sister spun, clutching his wrist-length sleeve with a vise-like hand. She pulled him forward, holding an accusing, trembling finger straight at him. Tiro traced the finger up her arm, following it all the way into a pair of frightful, unblinking eyes. He stumbled and placed his sweating palm against the wooden wall for support. "Sister...what's wrong?"

"Tiro," she began, a tremor in her voice, "what have you done?"

The knot in his stomach returned, the earth swaying in sudden lurch beneath his feet. "I don't-"

"*Tell. Me.*" She pulled him closer, tighter, her hand an iron fist that could not be shaken. "Do not play me for a fool!"

He steadied himself, resting an unsure hand upon her own. He breathed again, forced himself to speak. "I...I should have done it years ago. After..."

"After what? The first time? The second time? The tenth or twentieth times?"

Tiro dropped his eyes, the weight of shame a burden much too heavy. The hand upon his cloak loosened, so he squeezed it even tighter. She let it lift toward her cheek, leaning herself into its calloused palm. "Forgive me," he whispered, the words a painful reminder of his failure and cowardice through recent years. "I am sorry."

Her strong, sure hand returned to his, her other soft upon his face. "I know you are, Tiro." The first tear fell, his own, and Tara wiped the stray trail aside with a steady, loving finger. She took his hand and led him far to safety, where leaves and limbs let siblings mourn beneath their silent boughs.

*

"You're bleeding me dry, young man."

Tiro stiffened, relaxing when the man in shadow cracked a slow, sly smile. Although he had stood in the exact same spot many times before, monstrous waves of helplessness threatened to overwhelm him each and every time. The close, burlap walls of the officerial tent, the flickering candlelight, and the scowling guards posted against each wall didn't do much to alleviate the young boy's nerves. Being alone was one thing. Being alone, unarmed, and surrounded by hundreds of brute rebels was quite another.

He adjusted his tunic self-consciously, studying the man who had just spoken. His name was Hemas, a rough-looking captain of *The Hand* who seemed to take the act of rebellion multiple steps further than most. Whereas most in his order were clean-shaven and well kempt, Captain Hemas seemed to find the act of grooming much too tedious a chore in the wild. With a dark beard and mustache framing his lower face, and the hood of his forest green cloak hanging halfway down his nose, the man resembled a newfound species of hairy, prowling forest beast.

Clearly at home in the small, dank tent, the chief officer of the forest-shrouded rebel camp slouched comfortably behind a noticeably uneven bamboo desk. In one glance, Tiro unlocked the riddle of its apparent instability: littered across its surface were dozens of maps and blank parchment, half-empty bottles of thick black ink and numerous feathery quills. At the captain's right hand, atop a closed leather-bound book as large as any Tiro had ever seen, were five ornate throwing knives. The hunter gulped, wondered why a well-guarded captain such as Hemas needed not one, but five throwing knives so close at hand.

"Not that I'm complaining, of course." Tiro followed the captain's lifted hand, watching as the two imperial insignias from his last kill exchanged hands with a seemingly mute bodyguard. The similarly cloaked soldier crossed to the far side of the tent and opened a pair of thin wooden doors on a cabinet the height of a man. "But I do have to stop and ask myself why you're holding out. Wouldn't it be in everyone's best interest if you actually chose to join the cause? I mean officially, of course."

The boy cleared his throat as the crouching bodyguard noisily rummaged through the cabinet. "Forgive me, Captain, but I've always assumed my work and time were appreciated."

"Tiro, Tiro...it has nothing to do with that. Let's speak plainly with each other, shall we? You've brought a fair amount of attention on yourself. Too much, in fact. My superiors, for example, are starting to wonder if this is a one-way path, if you're only in this for the money." His eyes, hidden though they were, examined the visitor's every move, every gesture. "And if a man - or boy, as the case may be - were only in this for the money, how quickly could his motivations and loyalties waver?"

"That's absurd."

"Well, I know that." The captain leaned back, the sudden motion revealing the upper palm and top four fingers of the instantly recognizable markings worn by the well-known rebel group. The symbol, a simple outstretched palm, was the same dark shade of green as the cloaks each soldier wore. Movement stirred and the captain turned his head. The bodyguard crossed the room, placing a heavy rectangular chest in the center of the crowded desk. Hemas removed a key from below the heavy book, grimaced, and unlocked the chest. He returned his attention back upon the hunter, lifting the creaking wooden lid. "And you know that. But that makes only two of us - a rather insignificant number if you ask me."

"I risk my life each time I lift my bow," Tiro answered, the words he heard appalling. He lifted his hand toward the insignias somewhere safe within the cabinet. "After all of this, how could I possibly prove myself even more?"

"I've told you: make it official. For one, it would make everyone more comfortable if we could keep tabs on you. No one likes a ghost prowling the forests, aiming arrows at whomever he pleases."

Tiro froze, tried to swallow without the countenance of guilt. "W-what do you mean by that?"

The captain shrugged the question aside, counting out an impressive pile of shiny silver coins. His counting done, Hemas closed the lid, fastened the lock, dropped the coins into a small cloth purse, and resumed his comfortable slouch. "Besides, there is safety in numbers. Sooner or later, a trap will be set for the young ghost of a bowman raining terror on the Empire. You don't want to be alone when that happens, do you?"

He remained silent, the answer an obvious one.

"*The Hand* needs you, Tiro. Not as an enlisted grunt. Not as a pawn to move here and there at the whim of selfish officers. We need leaders of men, ghosts who can slink through daylight as though it were darkness. Hunters, prowlers...wraiths who haunt their every step."

The hunter's jaw jutted forward, his mind a bustle of activity. "I have always worked alone."

"Then it's time to work with others. Imagine,

Tiro," the captain added, unseen eyes cloaked in shadowed darkness, "what you and a team of five, ten, fifteen others could do for the cause."

The boy nodded, mentally applauding himself. He had risked his life for two long years to achieve this level of acceptance with *The Hand*. To be wanted, pursued, and admired were glorious crowns upon his head. "I will consider it, Captain."

"Please do more than consider it." He pushed himself from the table and stood to his feet. Tiro followed suit, making sure to stand as straight, as tall, and as upright as his tense back would allow. Hemas reached for the coin purse and tossed it gently from one hand to the other, walked around the cluttered table, and stood eye to eye with the young, experienced hunter. "One more thing before you go on your way: you delivered only two insignias. In my experience, scouts tend to travel in packs of three to four. So tell me, Tiro: were there two or three or four scouts in the forest?"

Ego deflated, Tiro's eyes fell upon the dark green symbol of *The Hand,* its fingers stretched wide across the captain's chest. He opened his mouth, the desire to save face paramount, and wove a subtle fabrication of the truth. The bowman's mouth closed; he heard the captain's breath loud within the tent and knew the man would surely pounce upon a lie. *Always proceed with caution.* "There were three, and I'm sure I hit each one. I was...momentarily preoccupied. Distracted. But I saw all three hit the ground. When I returned, only two remained. I found no stray arrows, no splatters of blood nearby. I truly don't know what happened."

"And you thought it wise to stay silent until prodded?" Hemas stared unblinking at the youth, watching the young boy's mouth open and close again. "Is there a chance he followed you home?"

Tiro relived the hunt, imagining it an impossibility. "No, sir."

"Did they see your face? Did you speak your name?"

His heart was a lonely star, its descent a fatal one from the heights. Reluctantly, painfully, Tiro nodded. "Both. And I revealed myself as *The Ghost*."

More perturbed than Tiro had yet to see, the captain shifted his weight from one leg to the other, pounding his thigh with the flat of his open palm. "Mistakes like that can kill you, Tiro. What's worse, they can kill an entire squad of men serving alongside you."

"I understand, sir. Lesson learned." He held out his hand, feeling the impressive weight of the thick coin purse fall into it with a pleasant metallic clink. He was ashamed, having never been more put off with a dual kill than he was in that moment. "I will learn from my weakness."

Captain Hemas nodded, pleased with the bowman's apparent maturity. "You'd better."

The hunter transferred the coins to his pocket, bowed his head to the captain, and exchanged candlelight for bright, glorious sunshine. Despite his shame, he breathed a sigh of relief, patting the added weight on his hip. His sister and mother would eat well that night and for many weeks to come.

Chapter Six

The sun journeyed west in a precise crescent and began its slow, fiery descent above Arach's sweat-laden head. From the moment the travelers made a hurried retreat from the haunted streamside, to the first conspicuous growl of a stomach foreshadowing sunset, Arach twisted and turned anxiously in the creaking leather-covered saddle. No sign of trouble nor premonition of impending visitation split the peaceful facade of an unconcerned traveler riding south. Each mile was a repetition of the last: the slow-moving cart lumbered ever forward along the right hand side of the free-flowing stream, never stopping, never ceasing.

"We'll need to stop soon," he spoke aloud, the sudden proclamation startling both man and beast. The traveler patted the dark neck of the horse and broke the tension with a nervous laugh. "I'm sorry, old boy. I'm afraid we'll both be a bit jumpy the next few days."

He looked up and slightly toward the west, estimating that sunset would arrive in no less than two hours' time. "My father told me tales of foreign lands where the sun never sets for months on end. Travelers eventually lose their minds in those places," he said. His hand wiped the sweat from his forehead and fell to his side. He turned his gaze from west to east, noticing the increasing amount of trees on the far side of the stream. "I don't care how hot it is, Yuzy. A sun-filled night with no moon, stars, or evening breeze would be a dream come true right now."

They traveled south for another half hour, spotted a lonely ancient ash tree not far from the stream's opposite bank, and decided it was as good a place as any to stop for the night. Arach pulled the horse to a gradual stop, unhitched the tired animal from its wooden burden, and made for the cart. He reached for his boots, pulled them on one after the other. He felt for any dampness in his cloak, found none, and finally, grabbed a handful of apples, salted meat as tough as his saddle, a few other odds and ends, and put them all in a dinged and dented black iron pot as old as dirt when his father was just a boy. "We'll sleep by the tree,"

Arach motioned with his head as he transferred the filled pot to his left hand and lifted himself back into the saddle. "I hope you don't mind staying saddled and tethered for the night."

The horse shook its head, clearly agitated, and its master tutted with the firm press of heels in its flanks. "Now, now. You know I wouldn't do it under normal circumstances." The pair reached the stream and Arach grinned as his companion splashed through the water a bit too haphazardly than was normal in a moment of apparent protest.

Upon reaching the far side, the traveler slid from the horse and removed a long, buckled strap from the bottom of the iron pot. He set the rounded cookware down, removed an apple from the same pot, and held the red fruit to the beast. "For your trouble, Yuzy," he said as the horse turned its head from the proffered snack. After a few moments standing there ignored, he set the fruit upon the grass, adding, "Very well, then. In your own time, old boy." He then proceeded to tie the strap around the rear legs of the animal, preventing it from bolting away on its own again.

Arach turned his back to the stream, placed both hands on his hips, and studied the landscape encircling him. The region was flatter than last night's horrific stop. Every stone's throw was home to at least one of the large ash trees, most a tad smaller than the one he'd spotted from a distance. The tree before him sat on a six-foot-wide gnarled truck of grey-brown color, two of its roots crawling above ground for the life-giving stream. Its branches, covered with no lack of leaves and twigs, stretched just as wide as it was high. Fungus grew from the northern side of the giant, as did a small family of edible mushrooms at its base. He smiled. It was a good place to call home for the night.

He circled the tree to collect as many dry branches as he could carry, more than enough to allow a moderate-size fire to burn throughout the night. The minutes passed quickly, the shifting shadows a constant threat and reminder that his one and only wish was nothing more than a rapidly diminishing fantasy. The sun, quickly descending toward the cart on the opposite bank, would tarry just long enough for him to set the fire and harvest a handful of mushrooms to serve as the base for a comforting pot of soup.

A branch the size of his old abandoned sword caught his eye. He retrieved it, returned with bowed head to the newly stoked fire, and sat with his back to the old gnarled tree. The fallen arm of wood was long, misshapen, heavy, and blunt, but offered more protection than he'd had all day.

The air shifted, turning putrid. He sat up with a start, clutched at the newly found weapon, and glimpsed Yuzy's mouth open and close noiselessly as it stumbled to the earth head first in a faint. "Show yourself, wraith!"

It appeared from the branches above, its translucent form dripping to the ground in multiple inky blotches, and floated just beyond arm's reach. "You think a stick can slay when blades cannot?" The branch turned to rot in Arach's hand and toppled into his lap like a pile of stinking wet debris. "You disappoint me. But tell me this: how did you know I was near?"

With breath held fast for fear of fainting, he averted his eyes, left the remnants where they lay, and pressed himself into the tree as far from the shifting darkness as was possible. When he exhaled, his breath turned to frost, vanishing after a momentary ascension. "I could smell you."

"Smell?" the being asked with glee. Legless, it moved forward and hovered before the shivering man. "And what do I smell like, Arach? Tell me."

His eyes lifted, staring in horror at the quivering tendril curled inside the dark swirling substance. For the first time, Arach noticed a pair of dull grey eyes glimmering faintly behind the emptiness and saw an indistinct trace of a veiled human form within. "Like death."

The deep, cavernous opening showed itself below the eyes, a smile of inhuman cruelty and malice splitting the lower portion of the head where a mouth should be. "Death? That, Arach, is not me." The tendril uncoiled itself and snaked its way across the stream with a series of small, nervous ticks. It paused above the abandoned cart and caressed the nearly vacant space in its rear. With dull eyes still fixed on those of the traveler, it cocked its head and sniffed at the air as a blackened tongue slid from the mouth to lick invisible lips.

Unable to exert his will over his body any longer, Arach emptied his stomach upon himself and the earth before collapsing to the ground with a sob and groan from deep within.

*

"Awake, man."

He opened his eyes to the dark of night, heard the crackling of flames in his ears. The pot above the fire hissed like the tormented offspring of the being waking him from a sudden restless slumber. Yuzy lay still beside the stream, rear legs twisted and tied with the leather strap, its tongue protruding from a partially open mouth. Arach stayed where he was, the temptation to move as dried up as the vomit on his face and neck.

"There is evil afoot, Arach. Do you know I've

never left your side while you slept?"

Arach rolled from his aching side to his back and squeezed both fists into his eyes. "Evil?" he spat before erupting into a humorless bark of a laugh. "You dare to speak of evil with me, wraith? And what, pray tell, is evil to a devil such as you?"

The being crossed the distance between itself and the man, appearing to crouch beside the prostrate human form. "One such as I finds evil in many places, Arach. Perhaps," it began before pausing in apparent thought, "perhaps one such as you would simply call it 'danger.'"

"Danger and evil are two separate concepts, you wretched monster. You, on the other hand, are both."

The apparition bobbed up, down, and side to side like a rotting apple cast into the flowing stream. "Forgive me, *human,*" it enunciated the last word for effect, "for I am older than the eldest of all your ancestors; I am more ancient than time itself, should time exist at all." It watched the man shift positions and raise both knees in the air, his back still flat upon the ground. "Thus I am sometimes confused - and even amused - by humanity's need to create words that failed to exist mere generations ago. Danger and evil; I fail to see any difference between the two."

"Is that what you're here for?" Arach asked as

both hands catapulted into the air above his prone frame. "Am I to be your language tutor?" Strength and furor rising like a storm-tossed tide, the man turned his head toward the being, his eyes a pair of daggers not so easily shattered as the first. "My stick, the one you turned to rot. I'm sure you remember that?" He pushed himself upright with his left elbow, grasping a handful of the dry shredded bark with the other. "In the right hands, a wooden stick could be a danger." Arach threw the handful of bark at the darkness, watching as it sailed through the figure unimpeded. "As for evil, when was the last time you looked upon your own reflection? Any man unfortunate enough to cross your bedeviled path could easily smell and taste the very evil that seeps from each and every pore of your accursed self!"

"What piercing words, Arach," it hissed in delight.

"Come," the man hissed in return as his feet made a quick path for the stream glimmering beneath a pure full moon, "and look upon yourself, wraith! Look!"

The shade shrunk and retreated from the invitation. "I know who I am, man; I don't need a reflection to remind me of that. Can you say the same for yourself?"

"You're a coward, then," Arach taunted,

unafraid.

"Never," it answered in a voice more unsure of itself than before. "But I apologize, for sometimes I forget how dear vanity, appearance, and outward beauty are to humankind than any other beast that roams the earth."

Arach crossed the distance between stream and unconscious horse in five short steps. He knelt beside the dark brown beast, placed a gentle hand on the ribcage rising and falling with slow, shallow movements. "Last night, it was this animal who felt your presence first. Before I had so much as a notion that you would appear, he knew. He knew! And he was terrified; so much so that he fled from my side."

"And you succumbed to fear because of its base animal instinct."

"I became afraid," Arach stood, an accusatory finger pointed at the slow-churning shadow, "because you tried to attack me in the night!"

"You lie," it answered. "*You* tried to attack *me*...and failed. Despite this fact, I brought no harm to you."

"You're twisting the truth, wraith."

"Truth?" The word was spat like viscous mud from its mouth. "Truth, reality, facts; are they all one and the same, or simply different words to control men and confuse a situation?"

"I'm bored with this worthless wordplay. Just say what you will and be gone already."

It grew again, blocking out the moon from the sky. The open cavern of a mouth grinned and salivated upon itself. "Tell me *truthfully*, Arach: if you saw an old, dirty beggar propped against the wall of a stinking tavern begging for help and dying of thirst, would you help him?"

Incredulous, Arach turned his back to the darkness to face the crystalline stream.

"Or let's say you found a young, beautiful woman in the same street begging for food and medicine for her dying father. Would you not run to her aid without a second thought? Would you, in your lustful human nature, not try to find her days later as your own wife lifted bloody hands in helpless defense? As her final cries of fear and pain carried just shy of a wandering husband's deaf ears?"

He spun on his heel and made a beeline for the hovering shade, ignoring the hideous gaping hole where mouth should be. "How dare you bring up my past, wraith! Are you trying to shame me? Guilt me?" he spat, the heat and flame of the waist-high fire reflecting violence in both eyes.

"Guilt?" it repeated with the same spine-tingling trill of a laugh. "Only a guilty man would deflect blame and accuse another of making him feel as such."

Arach raised both hands to his face, rubbed at the sudden flow from both eyes, and willed his pounding heart to steady itself. Defeat in his voice, he stammered, "I want you to leave, wraith. Now. And don't come back. I'm sick of your smell, sick of your presence, sick of your atrocious storytelling."

The being appeared to settle itself on the ground, shift in size and shape, and transform from the familiar oily shadow to a physical shape of a man conceived in subdued white light. "Look at me, Arach," it spoke, its voice a soft, pained whisper. When the traveler lifted his eyes, it continued, "Forgive me. I am only trying to help you, child. To bring you strength where strength has died."

He studied the glowing man before him and saw the hands held outward in a sign of openness and trust. He saw the regal clothing draped across a strong, powerful frame of indeterminate years. A small, jewel-studded crown encircled a head of white wavy hair, his hairless jaw clenched painfully below a pair of sorrowful, misty eyes. Arach paused at those eyes, feeling himself succumb to the emotion within. He wanted to let go of the pain, to free his deflated soul of the past the being understood so well.

Downcast, the traveler glanced at the

apparition's chest and saw a trail of the thick, oily blackness seeping through the kingly attire. The being peered down, wrapped the folds of golden cloth around his chest, and covered the horrific wound from sight. Awake as from a sudden stupor, Arach shook his head, snapping the fragile bond between ghoul and man. "Stop trying to deceive me, wraith. I told you to leave."

Tears fell from the eyes of the being cloaked in light, trickling down its cheeks and onto pale lips twisted in a false mockery of pain. Arach turned his face in disgust toward the stream, waiting for the paralyzing stench and faux light to fade. Alone again at last, he returned to the crackling fire and collapsed to the earth in sorrow.

Chapter Seven

He left the crowded rebel camp in high spirits and set his course for towering forest eaves and the village not far beyond. On two separate occasions, Tiro's westward path intersected with smooth highways, their dull grey cobblestones worn flat through recent years of constant imperial footfall. Although each wide public road beckoned Tiro to travel along the faster, straighter way, he cursed the misleading voice, continuing through dense wood and grassy field. After all, the forest was the familiar, safe route home.

Safe. Tiro felt he'd learned that simple truth a lifetime ago, the bitter taste ground deep into adolescent subconscious since the first imperial soldiers descended like fog from the north. The hunter knew he couldn't trust those plentiful easy-to-traverse roads where run-in after run-in with imperial troops was not mere possibility, but highly probable. Although no well-armored soldier would know Tiro was the lone ghost who haunted their brethren for sport, none would take too kindly to an armed bowman, openly hostile or not.

Tiro notched an arrow and opened eyes and ears to the audible whispers of a terrain waving him inward with outstretched boughs. His mind wandered to Tara, to his good friend Marik. Even in those reckless younger years, those peaceful times when wild-roaming children feared no man, beast, or soldier, Tiro knew the slightly older boy was a good match for his sister. He was faithful and hardworking, a trustworthy soul who had remained steadfast through chaotic, tumultuous years. Loyalty was his banner, and Tiro gladly waved it.

He leapt across a gently flowing brook, beaming at the image of Tara as bride, wife, future mother. She would flourish in those special, sacred roles, stretch her wings to become what she was meant to be. *One more month,* he thought wistfully, *and then it will be so. As for me?* Tiro rubbed the fletching of the arrow with his thumb, imagined himself a father, and laughed. The preposterous image faded into a hooded shade of himself, the forest-green hand of open rebellion stretched wide across his chest.

The hunter slowed his pace, letting the rattling chains of uncertainty drag his bow lower to his side. He smelled the air, squinting as he looked skyward. From where he stood near roots and stones, a wall of darkness crept slowly toward him, its churning mass a living, breathing vision of swiftly approaching nightfall. The smell at its corners tickled his nose, its scent an aroma of flames and wood and meat, the same prominent scent of a village settling in to a slow evening routine. He knew the village was close and wondered how the afternoon had faded so quickly into evening. "It can't be." Tiro felt his stomach, his trusted, most accurate gauge of time, and felt it, still and silent. He lowered the bow, the first hint of cautious intuition playing at his fingertips, and increased his speed.

The thick sheet of smoke came next, the panic shortly after. He pierced its dense, creeping boundary, in and through it like an arrow in a blinding morning fog, and ignored the sting of eyes begging swift retreat. He ran now, feet gliding across the dead, uneven forest floor, each step as sound and sure as a sprint across a barren flatland.

He passed the tree, that favorite resting place of his, its shadow passing like a towering phantom on his left; he began the precise countdown of trees, steps, stones, and seconds before the forest gave way to a clearing of wooden houses, walkways, and familiar village life.

But this time, life had failed. Tiro stumbled upon the first body - a headless, bloody thing tossed carelessly in the dirt - and kicked its companion piece with a stifled groan and sob. Incoherently, he cried out, each word running horrified circles from mouth to heart to head and back again.

The wall of grey mingled with violent shades of orange and red as darker, blacker columns connected earth to unseen clouds. "Tara!" he screamed and just as quickly bent at the waist, an uncontrollable bout of coughing seizing him by the throat. Harsh whispers of crackling, burning wood gave the only reply.

A wall collapsed, falling outward with a crash and ferocious expulsion of ashes and wood. The eerie outline of Marik's crippled house cut through the smoke, a haunting memory from childhood cast outward with it. Through smoke and flames, Tiro saw the first symbol clearly, those sickening triple brushstrokes of vain imperial victory displayed across the collapsing facade. His eyes moved from the cold, cruel markings to the gaping doorway, watching plumes of thick black smoke billow upward and far from sight. At the foot of the hellish doorway, a grotesque smear of blood welcomed any who dared approach. Marik's father sprawled headless there, sword not far from an open hand still stretched in hope. His body lay half in, half out of the flickering, spewing house, a last attempt to protect the ones he loved.

Fear and horror propelled Tiro deeper into the village. He passed another house, recoiling at the sight of blood, imperial markings, and countless burning corpses. "Forgive me!" he cried to each new body, tears of smoke, sadness, and shame coexisting in a pair of wide burning eyes. "It's all my fault! My fault!"

His foot stumbled again and he braced himself for the fall. The boy tumbled, dropped his bow and arrow, and felt a wet stickiness upon hands, forearms, and legs. Smoke entered his lungs and he lifted bloody palms to mute the painful cough. Tiro reached out for his bow and misplaced arrow, recoiling in shock as bloody hair and skin were all his hands could feel. He forced himself to look, willing himself to stay conscious at the sight of dozens of heads stacked carelessly in a cruel mockery of a pile. Each ghastly face wore a tale of final terror, each had a name he knew and cherished. "Forgive me," he wept. They were the only words that would suffice.

"Tara!" he tried, much weaker this time, in a fruitless attempt at a scream. He crouched as close to the earth as aching legs would allow, a painful posture benefiting breath, not sight. "Tara! Marik!" Again, his cries were hollow, unanswered.

A familiar wooden walkway came into view and, cautiously, Tiro reached out to it with a trembling hand. The boy mounted it, smelling heat and blood with each unnatural pull of his boots. The elevated path smoldered, burning his hands and feet while cooking the grotesque layer of blood upon its surface. He was helpless, vulnerable, but still moved forward. The hunter sheathed his still-strung bow and removed the dagger at his side.

The smoke began to clear as Tiro crept closer to the village center. Through the choking, man-made haze, he saw an outline. Even through the billow of smoke and fire, he recognized its shape, its size, its countless rough-hewn planks. Each and every nail had a story, a tale that he would someday cry for. He wailed in sorrow when he came near enough to see the wicked, mocking crimson red of the Empire etched across the last remaining wall his father built so many years ago. He stifled a scream with his wrist, the only recourse available to him.

Tiro glimpsed the body of his mother next, her long black gown of mourning half-burned and soaked through in blood. He found the rest of her in a collapsed pile of imperial trash, shed his cloak, and removed the head as carefully as his weak, frail body would allow. With his hands, he stroked the hair behind her ears, and placed the head upon his hooded cloak. He wrapped it lovingly - once, twice, thrice - and as gently as his convulsing body would allow. Through rough folds of cloth, he felt her nose, the prominent cheekbones passed down to daughter and son. Blood seeped through to trembling hands, but he cared not. Two hands lifted the head to his chest, a final parting hug, and upward to his face. "Ah, Mother," he moaned, numb lips wet with tears pressed flat upon her own covered forehead. "My mother...my only mother, please forgive me. I failed you. I should have done better..." Tiro cradled the head in his arms and placed it next to her body and the still-smoldering hut he'd helped create.

He passed each house, each fiery, crumbling building. Tiro inspected each mutilated body, each displaced lonely head. He wondered where Tara was, feared what shade of horror remained in eyes still wide from death's untimely final blow. He imagined her headless, shivering despite the untamable heat, and knew the face to look upon him would be the same scared face as his own. Perhaps he would lie next to her, take his own life once he found her. What else could be left in life for an orphan such as he?

In the distance, movement. Tiro froze amid the carnage, waiting for a lonely waft of smoke to clear. He rubbed his eyes, their warm flowing tears an unwelcome distraction, and had no trouble discerning those accursed triangular helmets through vision now unclouded. The bowman knelt to the earth, became one with the blood and gore, and took a deep stinging breath. Silent, he began to count.

"Seven," Tiro whispered and crawled on hands and knees to a blackened wall leaning outward at a precarious angle. He peeked around the corner, studying each soldier in his line of sight: one knelt much like him but held a brush in hand and silver bucket at his knee; another two held torches aloft, both men ready to eviscerate what few buildings remained; two officers stood with backs against a wall and swords in hand, both engaged in what appeared to be a heated discussion; lastly, another two stood watch over a huddled group of young female prisoners.

As smoke and orange embers floated harmlessly before his eyes, he saw the familiar fur-lined maroon blouse penetrate the dark, grey landscape around her. The boy said a heartfelt prayer of gratitude and wiped a newborn stream of tears from an ash-stained face.

Tara was shackled at the wrists to the others; a

long chain of girls bound one after the other. She shivered despite her sweat-covered brow, shook amid the plumes of smoke to left and right. Tiro spoke to her soul, relying on that sacred invisible thread connecting the twins, and willed the girl to lift her eyes. She did. Tiro mouthed her name, an inaudible sigh of sorrow, and she spoke his name to the air between herself and her twin. A soldier barked a gruff command and swung heavy fist down upon the girl. Through smoke, he saw the blood, saw her head snap back with a painful flail of hair and spit.

Anger welling as a fount, Tiro plunged his hand deep beneath its boiling surface, grasping the key to life and death. Vengeful, he withdrew it, letting the smooth black bow settle into his steady calloused hand. *Breathe,* he commanded himself, an order more taxing than expected. *Stay calm, Tiro. Focus.* He inhaled, exhaled. *Bringer of death. Giver of justice.* The bowman reached for the quiver, removed the first arrow and then the second, blessing each shaft with a sour kiss of hatred. *Steady my hand,* he prayed as he notched the first. *Steady the wind and steady my arm.* Back the string went, as far back as his blackened cheek, and trembled not. *Keep her safe.* His eye fell upon her bleeding nose, tracing a cold, calculated path to the armed coward yelling obscenities at his only living flesh and blood. *And give this dog to me*. He loosed his curled fingers from the biting, cutting string, felt its throb pulse up his arm.

The arrow split the air with a vicious hum, lodging itself in the small of the soldier's back. Tiro scowled, watching the armor-clad man turn, his face a twisted mask of confusion, and saw the glint of fire on steel as the arrowhead protruded through skin, stomach, muscles, and two layers of silver chain mail. The soldier reached down, mouth agape in voiceless horror, and stared aghast at the shaft's splintered and glinting head. Although overwhelmed with pain, still the man stood. Tiro moved on, knowing the shot was a perfect, lethal wound that would take minutes to run its excruciating course.

The next arrow was already on its way to the dying coward's colleague, this one a quick, painless shot to the head climaxing with a small spray of blood and grotesque flail of lifeless arms. Outcries and panic erupted, and Tiro made a silent retreat from the crumbling edge of charred wall to the opposite end of the burned out shell of a house. He cleared his head of ego and pride, inhaled, and chose his next target.

The first torchbearer fell with an audible thud, writhing in agony for a moment, and the second torchbearer met the same dark fate. Both flames flickered in the dirt, their treachery now complete, and lay ignored by the three remaining soldiers still in view.

The officers claimed his attention next. Tiro heard the two men calling out rushed, incoherent orders to soldiers still unseen and saw them begin to round up the shackled girls to make a hurried retreat as far from the burning village as the chaos would allow. He delivered the next arrow, hitting the officer in the upper thigh; Tiro winced, frustrated with the wasted shot blown slightly off course by an unexpected gust of wind. The man fell, though, and Tiro aimed his next shot for the officer's upper ear. He heard the sharp ping of metal piercing metal and knew the arrow had claimed its life.

More soldiers appeared, their uncountable numbers flooding smoky streets, the clink of heavy armor warning Tiro to escape. Possible success melted into certain defeat as shouts and screams of shackled girls co-mingled with taunts from well-armed warriors. Even still, Tiro raised his bow once more, firing straight for the symbol painter he had already marked for death. The can of crimson fell with a burst of red and a loud, sharp clatter. He watched the soldier fall, cheering the demise of the man and the cruel brush of imperial victory as blood and paint sprayed the wall, the shades between the two impossible to discern from where the hunter stood with bow still held aloft.

The thunder approached, its pulse rising from the earth as a stampede of soldiers loyal to the Empire ran for him with weapons drawn. Like waves upon the seashore they came, dozens upon dozens, and Tiro saw them split into thirds with calculated military precision. Twenty turned aside, surrounded the helpless chained girls, and began pushing them all toward a covered horse-drawn wagon. Wide eyes still fixed on the tide ahead, he reached inside his quiver, feeling the arrows that remained. *Five more,* he counted quickly. *My final task in life, my greatest, unpaid bounty.*

His words became his prayer, a prayer to become myth and legend as darkness claimed him for itself. It would be his last victory; a bittersweet one, but a victory nonetheless. Tiro grabbed the first of five arrows, drew the taut string back, and aimed at the incoming front line.

"Tiro!" he heard her scream, her voice the only sound that mattered in those final somber moments left in life. He looked up and saw her pushed, prodded, and herded into the wagon with the rest of the female captors. A wooden ramp was lifted, latched, and blocked them all from sight. A red canvas cloth was pulled down across the rear-facing ramp to seal the screaming girls inside.

All was lost. He wailed at the air, grief-stricken and hopeless, and lifted the bow for his final act of death. One last time he heard his name, a plea, a desperate cry for help. He stretched his soul out to hers and touched it with a final, loving caress. Tiro felt and heard her speak, the mournful words etched deep across his heart: *Don't forget me, brother!*

He lowered the bow, took a guilt-ridden step backward, followed by another. *I will find you, sister! Don't lose hope!* He turned his back to the onrush of soldiers and fled to the safety of wood and trees beyond.

Chapter Eight

He passed a sleepless night with his back to the tree and eyes lost in flames. An occasional waft of death's familiar stench reached his nose from time to time. Arach wondered if it was the prowling wraith or simply one of its recently deceased victims. Either way, the traveler knew he was not alone.

At last, the horse stirred. The unexpected movement woke Arach from his hazy open-eyed dream state and filled his heart with pity for the four-legged animal. He had witnessed animals pass beyond the threshold of death from grief alone and said a silent prayer the same would not be so for him. The beast was more than just a burden bearer: it was his one and only companion left in life, a friend of lasting loyalty if ever there was one.

"Another rough night, boy," he said as he pushed himself from the tree and stepped beyond the fire's edge. He knelt before the horse's head, stroking the fear and worry from the wide, dark eyes. After a minute had passed, Arach walked on hands and knees to the twisted rear legs and removed the leather hobbling strap. The horse lifted its head with a struggle, gained momentum, and kicked itself to an upright position with a painful-looking limp. "That's it. Good boy. How about a stretch and then a drink?"

Man and beast walked to the water's edge. Two heads plunged beneath the surface, reemerged, and shook the soothing, cold flow back into the stream where it was born. "Feels good, doesn't it?" Arach asked as he splashed through the knee-high water to the other bank. He lifted both hands to his head and rubbed the sides of his aching temples. As soon as he reached the lonely cart, he set both hands upon its smooth wooden edge. With a gulp, he envisioned the tendril snaking its way across the stream, pausing above the cart. . . Arach looked down at his hands, saw the blue veins bulging through tightly stretched skin, and clutched the cart like a man grasps for one last painful breath of life. *He has no control over you,* he chided himself, unsure if the words were even true. *Relax.* His body obeyed, allowed his quivering right hand to touch the flat of the wagon bed with a gentle caress.

A splash brought him back to the present with a jerk. "Stay there, Yuzy, I'm coming." He leaned into the cart, found the long, thick brush he had crossed the stream for. As soon as the familiar wooden handle with stiff black bristles came into sight, the horse neighed and stamped at the water in delight. Arach laughed, realizing it was the first time that glorious sound had escaped his lips in ages. "Excited, then? Good. We're due for a bit of excitement, don't you think?" He paused, reconsidering his words. "And not the terrifying sort. Something good. Something like this."

He dipped the brush into the stream and lifted its bristles to the horse's back, neck, stomach, and legs. He took his time, focusing on nothing more than the beast before him. "I don't think it's going to leave us alone, boy," Arach spoke in his companion's ear as he drew a final brush stroke across its neck. For the first time that morning, he took in his immediate surroundings. "Besides, I don't think we can run away from it. He's following us. Maybe even watching us right now."

Arach led the horse out of the stream by its reins. He reached for the black pot, now cool from the hours alongside the still-crackling flame, and brought it to the stream. He returned to the fire, doused it with one well-placed pour, and spread a layer of dirt across the smoking ashes. "But do you know what?" he asked as he collected the handful of items he'd brought across the stream for the night. "I have half a mind not to care."

The two stepped into the stream and came to a sharp halt as the ground began to shift. Unconsciously, Arach bent at the knees and held both arms parallel to the rumbling earth below, the stream a sudden birthplace of chest-high waves. He looked around and saw a pile of stones tumble and fall into the rapidly churning water swirling north to south, east to west. A snap to his rear caused the horse to dart for the far bank, but Arach's hand held fast within the reins. "Whoa, boy," he spoke above the rustle of leaves and limbs. A branch had split from the ancient ash tree during the quake, falling to the earth with a terrible crack. The large limb, the length of three men one atop the other, now rested in the very spot where Arach sat sleeplessly through the long dark night.

At last the ground settled, and an eerie stillness took its stead. In the near distance, the gentle sway of bark-covered pillars gave the only sign that the brief and sudden tumult was anything more than sleep-deprived imagination. He gave the horse a gentle pat. "Just a memory now. Only a memory."

They stepped forward and dry, firm land was

finally reached. Arach turned toward the lonely tree for a final parting glance. The being, in its original darkened form, hovered from behind the critically wounded ash tree. "Eyes forward, Yuzy," he whispered and quickly removed the cloak from around his tense, aching frame. "I've trusted you too many times to count; now it's time for you to trust me." He tossed the grey cloak over the horse's head, drew the sleeves back and across the pointed ears, and tied the makeshift blindfold as snug as possible. The beast protested, as any sane animal would, but the traveler grabbed the dangling reins and led his companion toward the waiting cart.

A crack and a groan drew his attention back across the stream. Although distance was his ally, it was fragile at best. While the span between man and wraith was vast enough for those dull grey eyes to vanish within the haunting shadow, Arach knew they were watching, waiting. He sensed them penetrate, wincing at their sting as psyche and sanity decayed with corruption. He felt an invisible tendril of despair claw its way into a heart unsteady with fear.

He lowered his head. "I'm going to strap you in, boy," Arach whispered, all willpower to resist the inhumane schemes of the wraith a dithering ebb and flow not to be trusted. "I will stay in front of you, Yuzy; I'm going to lead you. Understand?"

With trembling hands, he reached for the straps that would buckle the horse along both sides of the cart poles. With the temptation to resist too weighty a burden, he peered across the water once more. The wraith floated menacingly beside the downed branch, its invisible eyes turning the fertile soil of the traveler's infirm soul. "I will do my best, Yuzy. I'll find the flattest ground I can to make it easier on you."

Arach watched in horror as the tendril departed from its inky host and pierced the ground beneath. When the earth shifted again, the horse bolted two feet forward and came to a blind, panicked halt. "It will go away, boy! It will stop!" He glared across the stream and saw, rather than heard, the light-less being laugh. "We must ignore it for now. Do you hear me?" The traveler placed a reassuring hand on the horse's neck, feeling his own nervous quiver resound within the beast's cold, frightened flesh. "One step at a time. Simple as that."

He took the first step and heard the creak of the wheels turn behind him. "Good," he said. "Not so bad, is it?"

Another creak of wood was followed by a short but terrifying flutter. The orphan limb landed with an eruption of splinters in front of the procession of man, beast, and cart. Arach paused, lifted a hand to his chest to reclaim the stolen breath, and carefully directed the nervous horse around the new obstruction. "Don't look, Arach," he urged beneath his breath before succumbing to a subtle peripheral glance. On the far side of the stream, the wraith floated ten feet from water's edge, its path a precise mirror image of the slow-moving duo's.

It was with the fleeting glance that revelation dawned. "The stream!" Arach whispered, as newfound hope replaced the suffocating corruption. "I don't think it can cross. It's confined to the area on the far side of the water. To the east." He chanced another glance across the stream and studied the being floating noiselessly above grass and stone, its tendril hovering to and fro as if to sniff the air around it. The sight of the curling, oily extension of itself deflated his spirits just as quickly as they'd been lifted. "All except its arm, that is."

He continued further south, caution and concern for the blindfolded horse his chief priority. From out of nowhere, much like the arrival of yet another supernatural apparition, the base of an idea took root. "Whoa, boy," he called as he placed a calm, comforting hand on the nose of the beast. "I'm not going far; just a few steps to the edge of the stream." The horse kicked at the ground with both front legs, bobbing its blindfolded head up and down. "I'm still here, Yuzy," he added reassuringly, eyes cautiously affixed upon the hovering wraith a mere twenty-five feet away across the stream. "Just getting a drink of water, old boy."

"Come," it hissed.

Arach knelt in the dirt, feigning his best imitation of a man deaf and dumb to the horrors just before him.

"Come, Arach. The way is easier on this side. With me."

He ignored the hollow, haunting words as he dipped a pair of steady hands into the stream, letting the coolness reinvigorate his tilled, distraught soul, and lifted the makeshift cup to his mouth. The apparition churned and boiled within, raised its quivering tendril, and voicelessly commanded the evil extension of its self toward the vulnerable kneeling man. It hissed, cackling in horrid delight. The traveler swallowed his fear, watching the ghastly snake creep and twitch its way through still morning air. Closer it drew - ominous, imposing, frigid - until Arach could barely contain his wits and his nerves. He heard the sickening laughter, a cold, cruel song of victory for the haunting wraith, and blocked the grotesque sound and image from his mind.

And then the tendril arrived, so close he could

touch it were it a thing of solid mass.

He dropped his hands, and from the stream sent a shower of water skyward. An unholy shriek pierced the air and shook the ground with a quake more vicious than before. As the tendril retracted in a cloud of steaming putrid smoke, Arach ran to the stationary cart, grabbed the black pot, and returned streamside with a shout of boyish wonder. Heart pounding and ears ringing of excitement, he dipped the age-old pot into the water and hefted it out with a jubilant slosh. Frigid water splashed against his body and clothes, soaked him from chest to toe, but he welcomed the sensation as spasms of shivers echoed up and down his arms and legs.

The apparition seemed to suffer a similar but parallel fate, its emotion the exact opposite of the man shouting triumphantly across the river. It stumbled like a drunkard and shrieked again in pain, fleeing the edge of the stream as the retreating shell of a body grew frail and faint with each laborious inch of retreat.

Arach stood to his feet, lifted the sloshing pot, and placed it gently in the cart.

"You!" he heard, the hissing voice its weakest since the vile first meeting. "You are an evil man, Arach!"

He turned his face to the darkness unafraid,

watching the shadow fade to morning light. "Not evil, wraith." The traveler laughed in mockery. "Dangerous!"

Chapter Nine

The fluid wave of rushing imperials receded, reversing itself back into the ocean from whence it came. The lone bowman was just a boy, after all, nothing more than an insignificant nuisance in their bloodthirsty collective minds. Seemingly of one singular accord, they halted forward progress and let Tiro vanish unscathed, dense pillars of churning smoke erasing each and every trace of the ghost they'd let slip away.

Deep into the darkness he ran, the green of forest edge pierced not by airborne arrow, but by the sprinting boy himself. For hours, he ran and wrestled with himself before collapsing hard against a towering tree. He fell to his knees, hugged its massive, unkind trunk. *I should have stayed, should have killed more,* he argued with himself. *Nothing more than a coward.* He pounded his head against the rough bark, the act a useless attempt to clear a mind as cluttered as an attic full of boxed-up regrets.

Tiro felt the wind stir, heard it rustle the branches and leaves overhead. It became a whisper, a frightening chorus that caused his spine to tingle. The boy looked around, taking in the deep black of midnight and the climbing pillars of wood all around. In the darkness, he saw their faces - each and every one of the headless dead he'd stumbled across and wept for only hours before. The hunter knew their lives and their pointless deaths would haunt his days and nights so long as he had breath to give. He prayed for strength, that their deaths would not be in vain.

He lifted a nearly empty canteen to his lips, letting the liquid clear his throat still raw and burning from hours of smoke inhalation. Another gust across the treetops whispered soothingly and he was reminded of her. *Where are you, Tara? Where are they taking you?* The leaves continued their gentle song, a voiceless somber one, and Tiro's questions remained unanswered.

The boy pressed on, a slow-going affair under cover of darkness, and eventually found what he was looking for. Near the edge of a line of evergreens, he halted with caution, crouched beside the glade, and mimicked a soft trilling of a pigeon.

"Who's there?" The sounds of speedily drawn swords and retracted bows filled the cold night air. "Make for the torchlight, both hands in the air!"

Tiro did as commanded, made sure each step was as loud, scuffing, and grating as any human could ever manage. "It's just me. *The Ghost*."

Four rebel guardsmen dropped their weapons upon sight of the lonely hunter passing from darkness into flickering torchlight. "You're not kidding," the officer in charge of the western gate's night patrol answered. "We can usually hear nighttime wayfarers tromping through the woods a half mile distant."

The hunter shrugged, glancing from the shut gate to the handful of cloaked faces outside the eerily quiet camp.

"Weren't you just here this afternoon?" Tiro simply nodded, at a desperate loss for words. "Times are that tough, eh? You can't even wait until morning to redeem another bounty?"

Startled, Tiro lifted empty eyes from the officer's forest green symbol of *The Hand* to his face half hidden in shadow. "No. No bounties this time."

"Sorry, boy, but it seems these old, tired ears misheard you." The officer smirked, glancing at a pair of skulking soldiers, amused with the words.

"I could've sworn you just said you brought no bounties in. Not that I'd let you in this late anyway." He turned the single-edged sword in his hand, fingering its blade. "But we don't take too kindly to outsiders sticking their noses in camp under cover of dark while the captain is sound asleep; especially when said outsider has no imperial deaths to report. Just seems too fishy, you see?"

Torchlight fell across his wide dark eyes, orange-red flames reflecting brightly in the gleaming whites. "I don't care about bounties anymore, *officer*. But if you want numbers, then try seven. For seven men fell with my arrows lodged deep inside of their cold, dead bodies this day. And that, sir, is the least pressing news I have to give this night."

"Then spit it out, *Ghost*."

He took a step forward, ignoring the sound of retracted bowstrings from upon the wall. "I'm not a grunt for you to push around, officer, but a civilian. Last time I checked, it's our fields that fill your stomachs. Isn't it you who works for us? Therefore, I would suggest you wake the captain. Now."

"The arrogance!" the officer spat and waved the sword toward Tiro. "Do you know how easy it would be for me to stick you full of arrows and dump you into the woods, boy? Are you truly testing me?"

"Yes, I am." He took another step forward, eyes focused on the gate sealed shut just beyond the officer's back. "So wake him up or I will."

The officer placed a firm hand upon the hunter's chest, pushing him back with a shove. "You stay there, *Ghost*." He lifted his head to the wall above, nodded, and returned his hateful gaze back upon the boy. "This had better be worth it. If the captain kicks you out, you're a dead man. Hear that, boys?"

A chorus of grunts filled Tiro's ears and he shrugged each one off. For three minutes, he stood in deathly, awkward silence, looking from sneering face to sneering face.

Finally, the heavy camp gate swung inward and a hushed voice filled the emptiness: "He says to let the kid inside."

Tiro stood with hands on hips, glaring menacingly at the officer on duty for final confirmation.

"Well, you heard him, *Ghost*. Don't want to keep the captain waiting, do you? You know the drill."

He did. Tiro stepped forward, raising both arms to shoulder level. A pair of soldiers stepped from the shadows and removed his bow, quiver, and dagger. One patted him down from head to toe, stood, and added, "Now open your mouth."

Tiro obeyed, glaring at the smirking officer watching the uncomfortable proceedings. "You think I can hide a blade under my tongue and speak at the same time?"

"I was hoping you'd give it a try." He crossed his arms and dismissed the hunter with a curt nod of the head.

The visitor crossed the threshold and was immediately plunged into further darkness. The square rebel camp was constructed to be mobile, thus organized in such a way that teardown and construction were simplified. Hundreds of tents stuffed with sleeping foot soldiers, scouts, bowmen, and cavalry filled the areas to his immediate left and right; directly ahead and in the center of camp were larger tents housing officers of the rebellion, their aides, and a collection of stables along the north and south walls; to the rear of camp, which pointed east, were training grounds, a mess area, and more tents for the injured. The camp itself was surrounded by ten-foot-high walls of trees sacrificed for the good of the rebel cause. Every twenty feet or so were sentries posted along these walls, their fronts facing the surrounding forest, their backs all toward the inner camp.

"He wasn't too happy, you know," Tiro's armed escort chirped into the silence.

"The night watch officer at the gate?"

The soldier did a double take, stifling a laugh. "Well, Ensign Ewik's sour mood goes without saying." He chanced a quick but subtle glance behind himself toward the closing gate. "But I suppose that's all I should be saying about that."

"The captain, then?"

His escort nodded and continued in a whisper, "The cat's already out of the bag, bowman, but I'll give you a fair warning before you're shown in: if your visit could have waited until morning, you're in for quite the dressing down. Just be thankful you're not wearing one of these." He tapped the forest green symbol stretched wide across his chest.

Tiro ignored the useless warning, his concern for the captain's disrupted sleep of no concern to him.

They reached the well-lighted tent and found the opening pulled shut and flanked by two armed guards casting an unwelcoming shadow across the rough dirt path. Tiro's escort gave him a sincere nod, mouthing the words *Good luck*. "Your visitor, Captain!"

Captain Hemas stepped into view, holding the outer flap open for the young hunter. "Inside, Tiro." He eyed the two guards, shaking his head. "Just you." The boy obeyed, not cowed by the stern tone of the steely-eyed officer dressed only in a simple tunic and wide-legged trousers typically worn by coastal fishermen. He waved to a stool set back against the rough canvas wall and took his own seat behind the cluttered desk. Hemas leaned forward, eyes peering hard into the vacant opposite end of the tent. "A doctor from a local village visited me last week. I had him brought into camp so he could look over each and every one of my officers." Wiry beard and hair sticking out in all directions, the captain rubbed at both to smooth them out. His attempts unsuccessful, he gave up, setting his hand upon his lap. "Do you know what the doctor told me?"

Dumbfounded, Tiro merely shook his head.

"He said, 'Hemas, you are much too stressed.'" The captain's gaze slowly passed from the empty corner to the uncomfortable seated boy. "Can you believe that? 'Stressed,' he said. I wanted to slap the man and send him crawling back to his village without so much as a coin. I held my hand, though, Tiro, much as I wanted to give him the back of it." The bowman blinked, remaining mute. "Instead, I asked, 'What did you expect? I'm a rebel! A nomad! I wake up each morning with one goal: to hold a camp of men together as the Empire tries to whittle us down one sliver at a time. How can I not be stressed?'"

Tiro opened his mouth to speak and was

forced to close it just as quickly.

"You know what else the old doctor said? He said I should get at least five hours of uninterrupted sleep every night. *Every night,* Tiro! And here I am awake in the middle of the night, stressed beyond belief and newly awakened from a good night's sleep! What for? To humor the young villager who has no comprehension of courtesy and common sense!"

The hunter held his anger in check but noisily gritted his teeth through a tightly clenched jaw. He leaned forward, the fingers on each hand digging ten painful craters in both knees. "My village, sir, was burned to the ground. There is nothing left." He paused, observing the captain's countenance shift dramatically. "My mother is dead. I held her head in my arms."

"Tiro-"

"I am not done," he interrupted with an outstretched hand. "I watched as my sister - my only sister - and other girls were herded into a wagon like cattle. I could do nothing but watch. I don't know if she is alive or dead. So forgive me, sir," the words oozed thick with sarcastic flair, "if I interrupted your precious sleep. I'm sorry that I possess the nerve and wits of a boy who expected you to want a report as soon as possible." The bowman stood to his feet, reaching for the opening drawn shut. "Perhaps I'll just come back when it's more convenient."

Deflated, the captain motioned for the boy to sit, rubbed his beard, and steepled both hands in front of his mouth and nose. Tiro watched his head move from side to side, his shock and horror apparent. "My boy...I am so sorry. Forgive my abruptness and misunderstanding. You have my condolences." The hunter nodded in appreciation and forbade a tear to fall again. "These are cruel and evil men, Tiro. You have tasted bitter tears in the past, but now you have seen their heartlessness with wide unblinking eyes."

"But why?" Tiro asked, knuckles white as both fists clenched tightly at his side. "Why would they do this? Why my village?"

Hemas removed his hands from before his face, folding them on top of the desk as he leaned forward with a sigh. "Many reasons, Tiro, and none of them are easy or comforting."

"I don't care."

"Well...the escaped scout could have followed you home the other day. An informant could have revealed the location of their ghost." Color drained from the bowman's face and Hemas raised a hand, shaking his head with a grimace. "Listen to me, Tiro: you must not blame yourself. There can be none of that. Besides," he added, "these are simply two of many possibilities."

"Tell me others, then. I need to know."

Captain Hemas leaned back in his seat, soft eyes fixed upon the inwardly grieving youth. "Unpaid taxes. Simple domination, brute show of strength. Or perhaps your village was in an inconvenient location for their grander future plans."

"And my sister? What of her and the other girls?"

The officer's shoulders slumped. "The Empire prefers to keep most young girls alive. By *young,* I mean girls between the ages of seven and twenty years of age. This is what history has shown from the last twelve years of war, at least."

Tiro held his breath in anticipation of more information, but the captain remained silent. "And? What else? This explains nothing to me."

He took a breath, lowering gloomy eyes to the boy's clenched fist. "They sell them, Tiro."

"Sell? What do you mean?"

"You know what I mean," Hemas said, bracing himself for the hard truth to follow. "Some as slaves...others as whores. It all depends upon the buyer."

The room spun like a child's wooden top and Tiro thought he would vomit where he sat. He stood to his feet, crashed into a crate upon the floor, and picked himself from the ground. The hunter squeezed his eyes shut, the pain and movement in his head incapacitating. "Then we must leave!" He forced his eyes open and reached for the canvas flap of the tent. "If we could only hurry, sir, I'm sure we can find them." The boy turned back to the desk and saw the captain had not so much as stirred from his seat.

"Sit down, Tiro" He beckoned the young hunter to return to the toppled stool. The boy stood in place, immobile as a stone, and the captain stood to his feet, the heavy weight of leadership bearing hard upon his shoulders. Hemas crossed the distance between himself and the boy, reaching a father's gentle hand for Tiro's arm. "It's too late."

"I don't believe-"

"Tiro!" he squeezed the hunter's arm, bringing the boy to silence. "I have been fighting this war for eleven long years. I've lost sisters, cousins, aunts, and - God forgive me - my very own daughter. I would not lie to you." He paused, waiting for the distraught young bowman to lift his head. The captain met his hopeless gaze, peering deep within its depths. "She is beyond your reach, Tiro; in all likelihood, she will be on a ferry by noon sailing for some distant shore where folks like us are considered exotic. She is gone, my boy. I'm sorry. It's time to give her life over to God."

"God?" the desperate boy asked incredulously. "Is that whose name you dare invoke? *God?* Where is he and why would he care about me? He deserted me long ago!" Tiro mimicked the act of drawing his bowstring. "The only gods who have proved themselves faithful are Death and Justice! They have served me well thus far, Captain, and I will sacrifice all at their feet to save my sister."

Hemas placed his other hand firmly upon the boy's shoulder, plunging into his cold, dead eyes. "I understand your pain, Tiro. I have been to the same depths and back again more than once. And I had lost all hope for life until I channeled my hatred into this." He slapped the symbol on his chest with a flat open palm. "Now you must do the same. Stay with me, Tiro. Join our family. Be more than just a ghost who haunts the Empire's every step; become a wraith and train others to become like you. This is the greatest way to help your sister." He released the boy's tense shoulders, patting both with a firm hand of encouragement. "What do you say?"

"I say yes." Tiro raised his eyes, nostrils flared in anger. He gave a single sharp nod. "I will be your wraith."

CHAPTER TEN

"Well? What do you think?" Arach asked the unblinded horse. "Should we take a chance?"

The pair stood side by side and looked down upon a wide-open land. From the lofty perspective, the stream to their left took a sudden plunge in a series of cascading waterfalls before evening out to cut a serrated swath through the vast plain below.

Arach scratched his head and offered a sigh to the cloud-dotted sky above. It wasn't the trek down the rocky hillside that concerned him - it was the thin blue ribbon of smoke in the near distance. He looked to the heavens and studied the sun three-quarters into its precise path through the sky. The ground gave another rumble - the tenth such disturbance of the day - and the traveler's eyes darted quickly to the far bank. It was empty, had been since that morning. Even so, he didn't trust the emptiness. He knew he was not alone.

He considered the size and speed of his cart. Here and now, stealth was simply not an option. Sooner or later, the keeper of the distant smoky flame would spot him and be just as concerned with Arach as Arach was of him. *Perhaps,* he thought, *it would be wisest to make the first move*. Decision made, he nudged the horse toward a wide dirt path that wound itself back and forth, right to left, all the way down the edge of the rocky cliff to the flatlands below.

With both eyes focused on the sloping ground beneath him, he turned his ear to the rushing, splashing sound of water upon stone. It was more musical here than the previous miles he'd covered in days past. The traveler let its songs fill him, lift him, and erase the despair that filled his heavy heart; he allowed the bright, chiming notes to cheer his exhausted mind and body. *If the distant fire wasn't looming,* he thought, *or the evil wraith lurking, this would be the perfect place to make my bed for the night. Ah,* he lamented to himself, *to be serenaded to sleep tonight without a care in the world*. Fully aware of the despair refilling his soul, he forbade the depressing thought to settle in before continuing on.

The noisy creak of wheels alerted the stranger of his approach long before it came. Awaiting his arrival streamside was a weathered man wrapped in layer upon layer of various animal skins. A wiry beard hung down to his chest, a pair of smiling blue eyes the perfect complement to a friendly grin. He held a charred, twisted spit to the flame. On one end perched a rodent of some sort, its juices dripping with a pop as the stranger turned the long wooden stick. The man was alone, and he waved in welcome as the horse and rider came within a stone's short throw to the small streamside camp.

"Peace, friend," Arach spoke first with politely bowed head before chancing a look around the makeshift, cluttered camp. A triangular tent designed for only one person was erected, its smooth leather flaps cast open to reveal a short pallet and nothing more. The only weapons within view were a large unsheathed hunting knife beside the man and an unstrung bow propped crookedly against an edge-less cart smaller than his own. On top of the cart were an assortment of furs, skins, and small bags fastened shut with knotted leather strips. The man was a tanner - a rather successful one by the looks of it. "I spotted your fire from the ridge above and thought it best to make myself known."

"Welcome." He bowed his head kindly in return. "I was hoping you would come this way. It's been a week or more since I happened upon anyone else out here." He pointed to the sun still lingering in the sky above. "Not much light left, is there?"

Arach grinned crookedly and slid from the top of the beast. "Not much at all. Would you mind having a guest and his horse for the night? I have a bag of apples that would go quite well with that meat of yours."

The stranger looked quite pleased as he nodded and gestured for Arach to take a seat beside the fire.

He untied Yuzy from the cart and led him a short distance away from camp where the stranger's mule stood stock still, its head buried in a bag of oats. He hobbled his own horse, gave him a pat, returned to his own cart for the bag of apples, and sat beside the fire. Arach motioned toward the stranger's cart. "Business is good, then?"

"More or less. But right now is just the calm before the storm. Another two months or so and I'll turn south for the larger towns as winter sets in."

Arach nodded, handed the stranger an apple, and kept one for himself. "So you're familiar with the area, then?" He watched the man nod and take a bite of the fruit. "Ever seen anything...odd? Out of place?"

The stranger devoured the apple, looking at the bag with unveiled interest. Arach stood, returned with both arms full, and handed him another two. "Thank you, ah-"

"Arach."

"Thank you, Arach. And I'm Rimmel, by the way," he added with another bite. "As for oddities, well...I've seen many an odd thing here and there from time to time. Animals where they shouldn't be, a few unusual deaths - things of that nature. Sometimes, I see things in the dark, but I attribute those to being alone for weeks on end, you understand?"

He let the tanner laugh and finish the second apple. Arach studied the stream and land beyond the far bank, unsure if he could ever broach the subject of the darkness haunting him. "Yes, I can understand that."

"So I assume you're not from around here, then?" Rimmel asked as he looked the traveler up and down. He removed the meat from the fire and stuck the end of the stick into the ground to cool.

Arach shook his head. "No. I've come from Fiyimi across the sea." He leaned forward with a sigh. "On my way back now."

"Fiyimi," the tanner repeated with a nod. "A beautiful place, I hear. But I've also heard there's trouble brewing out that way."

Arach nodded through the silence.

"So what brings a man all by his lonesome into

the wild and middle of nowhere, Arach?" He removed the rodent from the stick, halved it as best he could, and handed the larger portion to the traveler, who accepted it with gratitude. "Or maybe I shouldn't pry. Forgive me, my friend."

He turned the morsels of meat in his hands, his appetite suddenly diminished. "My wife was from a village northwest of here. Borvea, if you've heard of it." The tanner nodded as he chewed the meat and licked his fingers. "Once upon a time - a long time ago, mind you, not long after we were married - she asked me to take her home...after she had passed."

Rimmel's hand dropped, the half-eaten carcass with it. "I...I'm sorry, Arach. Accept my condolences."

He nodded, appreciative of the heartfelt sentiment.

"That's a long journey for any man - even to keep a promise from years ago when love was young and new. She must have been a wonderful woman."

"She was." He rubbed his head, the sudden throb between his eyes nearly debilitating. "Her family has a piece of land outside the village. Very beautiful place. Very peaceful, which is hard to come by these days. At least where I come from."

Rimmel watched the traveler for another

moment in silence. "Was she sick?"

Arach shook his head, perturbed by the intrusion into memories too close and painful to relive. Nevertheless, he was strangely grateful for the chance to speak his mind with a random, fleeting stranger passing in and out of life. He reached for a nearby stick, twisted it unconsciously between his fingers. "I was away from home one afternoon. Gone much too long, if truth be told. When I returned, the front door was hanging by its hinges, the place a complete mess. Of course, I knew something was wrong as soon as I turned the corner. But then I stepped inside. She was there." Try as he might, he couldn't continue. He closed his mouth, turning his face from the flickering flames.

Rimmel leaned forward, forearms on his knees. "I assume they found the thieves, though?" he asked in genuine concern.

He tossed the twisted stick into the fire, watching it blacken, burn, and disappear. "They were not thieves. They were soldiers."

The ground quaked again, bringing both men to their feet. "You asked about oddities," Rimmel said, his attention now on the collapsing fire pit. He reached for a bucket of water, holding it aloft just in case. "Well, we've been having these tremors all day long." He shook his head, breathing a sigh of relief as the ground settled and became still once more. "I don't remember the last time we had a single quake in these parts, much less a day chock full of them."

Arach glanced across the stream once more, scanning the length of rocky bed and the darkening horizon beyond.

"You keep looking around," quipped the tanner as he placed the bucket on firm, unmoving ground, "like you're expecting something to be there. What is it?"

"It's passed, boy," Arach called to his terrified horse and returned to the fire. The tanner studied him, waiting for an answer to the question. "It's nothing. Well...I don't know how to explain it, exactly. For two nights, something followed me on the far side of the stream. But it never crossed the water and I haven't seen it since this morning. Perhaps it's lost interest in me."

"Perhaps," Rimmel seemed to agree as he returned his attention to the unfinished rodent. "But a stream ain't much protection against wild men or most animals. And that's why I stay close to my old trusty friend here."

Arach nodded and settled in beside the fire as he watched the tanner pat the ground beside the deadly hunting knife. He heard the sound of his old knife splintering and shattering into a hundred useless pieces in the hillside, hoping the wraith would stay beyond sight and sound that night. He was sure Rimmel would throw or use the blade in vain and imagined the fate of a traveling tanner without a knife to cut or skin his livelihood.

"Anyway...I'm sorry, Arach," Rimmel continued to the bewilderment of the traveler. "For your wife, I mean. Such a pity." Arach declined his head in thanks. "They say the Empire is growing bolder on the mainland. Not so much in these parts…not yet, at least."

"It will happen, Rimmel. It's in their blood, inevitable."

The tanner swallowed and shook his head. "So what will you do? You said you're going home. Why? For vengeance?"

His laughter erupted without thought, devoid of humor. "No. Not for vengeance." He reached for the chunk of meat, wiping the dirt from its recently cooled surface. "I must return home because it's the only thing I can think of to do. Besides, what good is a single man against the might of an empire?"

"You can always join the rebels."

Arach took a bite of the succulent meat and let the juice run down his beard. His head shook. "No. Not them. I feel like another purpose awaits."

"Such as?"

He shrugged and took another bite.

"Where I come from, it's a man's duty to avenge his woman." The tanner flinched, recognizing that his words were terribly harsh for a man he'd only just met. "Forgive me, Arach, I meant no offense. I meet so few men in the wild these days, I fear I've slowly lost my sense of tact."

The traveler dismissed the words with a wave. "No offense taken. I have friends who've joined the rebels. Men who joined for a noble cause. But I've seen them, Rimmel, after they've returned home from weeks, months, and years on the *frontlines,* as they call it. I've seen them strut about in their forest green cloaks, seen the way they flaunt their sacred symbol of *The Hand*. I've seen what their cause has done to their easily twisted minds. The very men who swore to defend our land against the 'evil empire' have betrayed the same people they've sworn to protect - my wife being one of them." He paused in painful recollection. "Do you know what they told me after I found her in a pool of her own blood? After I cleaned her battered and bruised body, dressed her to hide the deep triple markings of a king mad with unquenchable bloodlust?"

His only answer was the steady crackling of flame.

"I was told, 'But, Arach, if only you'd chosen to pay the protection fee we'd offered time and time again!' As if I was to blame for the actions of cold, heartless men." He turned his head in disgust and saw the sun half-hidden on the horizon, the sky a brilliant amalgamation of reds, oranges, pinks, and purples. "You ask if I will join the rebels. Well, my answer is an emphatic *no*. Never. I will not desecrate the memory of my wife in such a way as to ever join those hypocritical men. Today, there is no better side to stake a claim with; no king or ruler or judge to run to for justice. If you ask me, the Empire and the rebellion are simply two sides of the same corrupt coin."

Peace settled upon the land and he prayed that it would last. "No, there are no victors where I come from, Rimmel. We can toss that coin a thousand times and never find ourselves the better for it."

The sun said farewell to the day as both men studied its swift, fiery descent in much needed silence.

"I'm so sorry," the tanner eventually muttered without looking toward his guest.

"So am I."

Chapter Eleven

He was an apparition - alone, invisible, ignored. He held a crude handmade bowl at his side and nervously tapped his thigh with it. When the line moved forward, he lifted the smooth wooden thing up and forward with outstretched palms and felt a slimy lukewarm splash against the skin of his hand as a white haired wrinkly old man spooned the sloppy mess into the bowl. "What's in it?" Tiro asked as he wiped the glutinous residue from the back of his hand. The cook dipped his cracked ladle into the stinking pot once more, served the next man in line, and stared blankly into a faraway invisible realm. "Okay, then."

The newcomer shuffled left and studied his next two options: piles of moldy bread or paper-covered mounds of rock-hard rice. Both looked weeks old at best. He grabbed a stone of rice, removed the paper one torn fragment at a time, and dropped it in his bowl with a stomach-churning, oily plop.

Tiro turned his back to the crowded mess line, facing the next awkward stage of the dark unknown. There were no tables in the open camp clearing, no seats to claim while waiting for other hungry colleagues to congregate and fill each empty space. Instead, pockets of men clustered in small-to-medium groups on foot or seated cross-legged in the trampled, worn down grass. The simple act of forward progress was more nerve-wracking than Tiro had expected. Choosing a free seat among many was simple enough. Choosing a closed-off group to join was a conscious, specific decision. He would be the clear outsider, the nameless intruder penetrating the ranks of an already-established clique.

Just move. His feet were weights, dual anchors holding his upright frame staunchly in place. He cut the cords - first one and then the other - and stepped forward into the great unknown. Rudderless, he drifted to the nearest island, hoping beyond all hope that the mass of men would cast their ropes and kindly pull him in to shore. So many backs were turned toward the young newcomer, but Tiro attached himself to the small cluster's edge, dropped both eyes to his unappetizing breakfast, and busily mixed the mess of food into a slimy consistency devoid of any tooth-shattering bites.

"-so we set each crushed head alight and hurled them all across the walls." Tiro lifted his eyes to match the voice with a face. On the far side of the small circle of fifteen men, a fair-skinned, red-haired westerner smirked as the rest of the group laughed. The man took a large, painful-looking bite out of a fist-sized loaf of bread and pointed the remainder north. "We fell back into the woods til nightfall, which was plenty of time to let them mourn and let the panic set in. I believe we let two watches pass before we surrounded the town and lit torches. The town was an inferno before the sun had even risen."

Tiro let the mishmash of murmurs die down and tossed his voice into the fray. "Where was this?"

All eyes turned toward the unfamiliar voice. The westerner dropped the half-eaten loaf into his bowl, looked him up and down not unkindly, and answered, "What's this? A newcomer? You snuck up on us, young man, which is quite a dangerous habit among so many armed and bloodthirsty men!"

"Forgive me." Tiro shrugged, a mischievous grin breaking the corners of his mouth. "Some habits are second nature."

"So long as you keep your habits away from our soiled underclothes, we should all be fine," another fair-haired man who was squatting on the balls of his feet chimed in to the amusement of the others. Tiro cast his laughter into the chorus and took his first bite of the slop. He swallowed, realized it wasn't as bad as he'd feared.

"No, the boy doesn't look the sort, Zed," the red-haired man added in reply and turned to study the new face. "What's your name, young man?"

"Tiro."

"Welcome, Tiro. I'm Commander Cephan. Have you heard of Attanabury?" The hunter shook his head and lifted a makeshift spoon to his mouth. "It's an Empire-controlled town five days' ride northeast of here. Just on the border of where all the real fun and games begin if you're looking at a map."

Tiro felt himself shrink to the size of his bowl at the words. He had never seen a map, never traveled any further than a half day's trek from the village he'd grown up in. For him, the world revolved around home, the forest surrounding his village, and the handful of small market towns scattered along three regional Empire-controlled thoroughfares. He swallowed the mouthful of lukewarm soup, knowing those days were now his past.

"So what brings you to *The Hand,* Tiro?" Cephan asked. Fourteen pairs of eyes traveled from the red-haired man to the dark-haired boy. "Free food? A life of excitement and adventure?"

"I-," he began as memories of smoke, fire, and blood filled his nose and mind. The bowl of half-finished soup dropped from chest level to stomach level, its contents as good as forgotten. Tiro raised his eyes to the wooden wall dotted with sentries, to the tops of swaying trees beyond. In the distance, a thin trail of merciless black smoke. He took a deep breath through his nose. "Today, I have nothing left."

His gaze dropped from the heights to the sober men encircling him. They nodded - almost as one - and set eyes of empathy and understanding upon him. A new voice spoke, its compassion deep and true. "You are not alone, brother. Welcome home."

A chorus of agreements echoed softly, filling his heart with newfound purpose.

*

Tiro's pulse pounded audibly in his neck, chest, and ears, an uncommon feeling for the boy crouched quietly behind a slightly curved waist-high wall. Somewhat distracted, he cleared his head, breathing in and out. His right hand reached for the quiver and removed three black arrows. Slowly, he reached above his hooded head, placed two of the long, straight shafts along the lip of the protective wall. Quietly, he pivoted, left knee pressed down upon the earth, and grasped the familiar bow in his gloved right hand. First arrow notched, he visualized the field before him. With a slight turn to his right, he stood to his feet, drew the bowstring with little to no effort, and let the arrow fly. Before the familiar *thunk* had even filled his ears, the bowstring brushed his cheek and sent another arrow eastward. One more *thunk*, another pull of the string, a final hum through the air, and the pleasing sound of the third arrow came to a sudden, abrupt stop.

He exhaled, dropped the bow to his side, and studied his glorious masterpiece. Applause filled the air, its hypnotizing drone ricocheting against the far camp walls. The bowman turned, acknowledged the sound with a nod and a raised hand.

Captain Hemas stepped from the crowd of men, his applause as enthusiastic as the rest. "A thing of beauty, Tiro!" The officer lifted a gloved hand to his forehead, squinted in the sunlight, and studied the three small circular targets spaced ten yards apart and fifty yards distant. Each arrow had found itself a new home in the center of each pockmarked circle. "Accuracy is one thing. Accuracy with impressive speed is quite another. I wouldn't have believed it if I hadn't seen it for myself."

Tiro nodded, pleased with the compliment.

"So tell me: how did a young boy from such a small village learn to shoot like that?"

He looked downfield, visualizing the years of training since his father's brutal death. "I suppose I had plenty of free time on my hands." *That and an unwavering desire for revenge,* he thought but held his tongue in check. The boy removed an arrow from his quiver, held it parallel to the ground, and studied its beauty - the lines and the angles, its smoothness and sharpness. "When I was younger, I was a climber. I would run to the forest, climb trees, and sit there for hours each day. I became silent and invisible, and learned how each animal moved along the ground to hunt its own prey.

"My mother worried about me, though. She told me I should do something with myself. 'So long as you're out there,' she said, 'you should at least try to bring something back to eat!'" His mind wandered to the last image he owned of her: that of a bloody and headless victim cast heartlessly to the earth like a rotten, fallen tree. He tried to clear his mind, only partially successful. "But I had no desire to hunt. Instead, I would climb into a tree and pick an animal off from the heights. It was the first thing I'd do each morning. Then I would climb back down, gather my arrows and newly killed dinner, and return to the branches for the rest of the day. My goal was to become better and faster so I could sit in the trees and think for longer." Noiselessly, he returned the arrow to the quiver.

"About him?"

There was no need for clarification. Tiro nodded.

"I never had the chance to meet your father, but I've heard plenty of tales about him. He was fearless, a born leader. Did he ever tell you stories of his days in *The Hand?*"

The boy shook his head. "When he came home once or twice each month, he always said the time was ours alone. Not once did he ever speak of work...or whatever it is you call all this."

The captain grinned knowingly and leaned against the short wall, watching the mass of soldiers make a silent retreat from the training ground. "He was captured once. Chained and sent deep into the dark land up north. Back in those days, if one of us was captured, we were tortured and hung from stakes along the roads. They'd hang us for miles, one right after the other, and just leave us there for months on end."

Tiro swallowed hard. It was a fate he'd never heard mentioned before.

Hemas chuckled, acknowledging the relaxed salutes of a group of departing soldiers. "They don't do that anymore, though. Perhaps they found it to be a waste of resources and man-hours. Anyhow, your father was chained and on his way to a cold, brutal death when he staged an uprising of prisoners. With his chains and bare hands, he slaughtered his captors, escaped through enemy territory, and made it all the way back to camp. He and the eleven others he'd saved walked, ran, and crawled nearly thirty-five miles on that long journey home. All of them weighed down by chains and starvation, no less."

The hunter stared in bewilderment at the captain as wellsprings of pride and emotion drowned all attempts at coherent speech. He cleared his throat and found his voice. "But he never said such a thing. Why would he hide something like that from us?"

Captain Hemas grinned, looking upon the new recruit with a bemused eye. "Here is your first lesson, Tiro: a good soldier never tells his woman what happens in war. Lesson Two is similar: a wise soldier likewise hides this information from his children, for he knows they will turn around and tell their mother."

The two men shared a laugh, Tiro nodded in sudden enlightenment. "Do you have a girl?" He saw the newcomer shake his head, glanced beyond the boy's face, and nodded at a soldier approaching from behind Tiro's right shoulder. "Enjoy your days as a bachelor while they last, then, for life will rarely be so simple. And when the day comes for you to shackle your fate with another, remember the following words: the fastest way to get yourself killed is to confide in her about all of this." He waved his arm around camp with a flourish. "Women are all the same, Tiro, and their methods are not unique. If you tell them about your life as a soldier, you will find your time on earth has been mysteriously shortened. Some will strangle you and others will beat you. A few may tie you up and leave you for dead, but most will incessantly beg you to come home and just plain nag you to death."

Tiro felt the weights of life slowly ascend from heavy shoulders. "Thank you for the advice, Captain, I needed an honest laugh. I will take your words to heart."

"Good, good," he answered as he straightened his posture along the training wall. "I'm only half-joking, of course."

"Now, now, Captain. Don't tell me you're handing out advice about women again."

Tiro nodded his head at Cephan's approach, watching as the captain raised his own chin with a hint of a grin and sparkle in his eyes. "Just a little soldier to soldier advice for our latest recruit." His attention returned to the hunter as before. "His name is Tiro. Please tell me you didn't miss his training exercise."

Cephan brushed his cloak aside, tucked both thumbs into a belt at his waist, and nodded in greeting. "We met at breakfast this morning and no, of course I didn't miss the *spectacle* you mistakenly referred to as a *training exercise*. I just about lost my voice and my temper, trying to get the men to settle down and stop yelping like a pack of wild motherless children."

"Ah, but do you blame them?" Hemas asked, his eyes flitting from one man to the other. "When was the last time you and I, much less the men, saw such a show from a new recruit?"

The red-haired westerner pondered the question for a moment before shaking his head with a frown. "Unless you're counting me, then never." He brushed the captain's amusement aside and turned his attention to Tiro. "Most newcomers are nervous and spooked with so many eyes on them. But you, Tiro," he wrapped an arm around the hunter's shoulder, giving him a firm pat on the chest, "you handled yourself quite well. The captain here must have acted on the wisdom of the gods to have brought you into the fold so quickly outside of open recruitment. Yes, I'll go ahead and say it: it was a stunning display of genius, Captain. Absolutely stunning."

Feigning annoyance, Hemas stroked his thick dark beard, placed both hands on his hips, and sighed dramatically. "You think I can't see through the phony flattery, Commander? Perhaps you should just tell me what it is you want before I tire of standing here listening to these pathetic attempts at groveling. So spit it out. Make it quick and be on your way."

The commander declined his head briefly and held an outstretched hand toward the hunter. "I want him, Captain. And to be honest, I know the rest of my colleagues are lining up at your tent right about now to beg the very same favor. In truth, I simply thought I'd try to get first dibs at the boy. Show some initiative, you know?"

"Initiative?" Hemas repeated mockingly. "Perhaps the word you seek is *greed*, Commander." Both men laughed, Cephan shrugged, and both looked to Tiro, still standing mute. "Very well. Take him out on patrol with you. Let him get his legs under him, see how things are done." He looked the younger man up and down. "But don't tether him down, Commander. Give him a measure of freedom, see where it takes him." He clapped his hands together, took a step backward, and added, "I'll expect a report as soon as you're back."

The two men still standing near the half-wall saluted the departing captain and faced each other. "What do you say to that, Tiro? Are you up for some action?"

Excitement grabbed hold, lifted him from earth, and filled his lungs with new, pure air. He hefted the bow, tugged briefly at its string, and let his enthusiasm loose with a burst of sudden untamed laughter. "Yes, sir. I am ready." He focused his energy, hatred, sorrow, and strength into a single point within, envisioned vengeance for his sister, and steeled himself for the task ahead. "So long as justice is in the balance, I will always be ready."

Chapter Twelve

"Wake up!" The command went unheard and Arach was jarred from the realm of unknowing by a swift kick to the upper thigh. "Wake up!"

"I'm awake already!" He deflected another blow to his midsection and rubbed the sleep from his eyes. "Don't do that again. A simple nudge would suffice."

"I tried. It didn't work."

Arach studied the tanner, searching for any trace of humor in his eyes. There was none. "What is it?"

Rimmel left the curled-up traveler where he lay beside the crackling fire and squinted in the opposite direction of the stream. "It's the animals. They're spooked."

Begrudgingly, the visitor pulled himself to an upright position and looked beyond the fire to the field. The tanner was right. “Yuzy,” Arach called as he stood to wobbly feet and brushed the dirt from head, hands, arms, and sides. He left the warmth of fire, spotting the gleaming eyes of the panicked beast. “I'm here, boy. What do you feel?” As the distance shrunk from meters to feet to inches, the traveler circled wide enough to approach the neighing animal from the front. The horse was clearly spooked and the last thing Arach wanted was to startle his companion any further.

He dropped his voice to a soft, hushed whisper, resting his head against the beast's right cheek as his hand caressed the other. “What is it, Yuzy? Is it our old friend? Has he drawn near?” Arach lifted his head as the horse nuzzled against his heaving chest in fear. He squinted in the dark, a fruitless search for the stream's far bank. The furthest he could see was its near edge, its shallowest depths twinkling in the dim firelight. He faced the tanner. "Did you see anything?" The fur-wrapped man shook his head. "Any quakes?" Another no. The inevitable reality began to sink in and he lifted his strained, sleep-deprived eyes to the sky in search of the moon. The silver disk had vanished, its nighttime path trampled beneath a thick caravan of unseen clouds. "Any idea how many hours remain until dawn?"

"You'd only just fallen asleep," Rimmel

answered. "Six hours yet is my best guess."

The traveler winced, scratching at his unruly beard. "Perhaps we should fill some buckets with water, keep them close at hand." He spotted the naked blade upon the ground, adding, "And don't be too quick to rely on that for safety."

Confusion crossed the tanner's face and he reached for the knife despite the cryptic warning. "You've been a bit too paranoid since arriving, my friend. Now don't get me wrong," he gestured, both hands outstretched, "I know how it is to travel alone in the wild for days on end. But I'll be needing some answers right about now."

Arach left his horse's side, making for the bucket lying empty near the crackling flame. "That makes two of us," he muttered under his breath and crossed the distance to the sandy bank. It was dark and bleak, and still he couldn't see beyond mid-stream. He returned his attention to the befuddled tanner, cleared his throat, and beckoned him streamside with outstretched palm. "Do you mind giving me a hand? Could you fetch a torch and shine a little light over here for me?"

Rimmel reached for a cloth-wrapped stick, held it over the hungry fire, and watched as orange tongues licked voraciously and consumed the upper portion of the torch. The tanner took a step toward the bubbling stream and began again. "As I was saying, Arach-"

The words were cut short as the all-too-familiar rumble of earth and stone split the tanner's statement in two. Arach fell to his hands and knees, staring in wonder as the sand vibrated, shifted, and bounced stones and pebbles in a race across the groaning, bouncing earth. He felt the sting of heat, spun in place, and saw the tanner on his back, the torch jumping across the sand in an awkward stuttering motion. Arach returned his focus to the stream and caught a haunting reflection of panic and fear. He flinched before recognizing the shadowed face as his own. He dismissed the frenetic emotions, reached for the torch bouncing playfully toward the water, and held it aloft. Another reflection this time, one of darkness and corruption on the far edge of stream and sight. "Rimmel!" he cried, afraid to pry his eyes from the unwelcome guest. "I think you should leave! Gather your things," Arach began and fell at the edge of the current as the glimmering tendril struck downward into grass and soil, the upheaval that followed the worst of the day so far, "and leave me be!"

Without so much as a farewell, Arach saw the tanner rise and run for the presumed safety of fire and light. The hurried, imprecise clatter of frantic packing filled his ears, an oddly reassuring sound to the traveler as he stood face to face with the being across the watery gap. From the earth the tendril rose, twitched, and paused midair as if in undecided limbo. "Leave him, wraith," Arach hissed into the night and chanced a glance at his feet where he'd left the empty bucket. It was gone, lost in the quake, and he dismissed the sinking feeling of vulnerability within. "Isn't one man's life more than enough for these foolish games of yours?"

"Games?" the apparition asked and dropped the inky extension of itself to its side. "This is no game, Arach. But perhaps a game would be an amusing time-killer of sorts, would it not?"

"Games are for children." Arach glanced backward toward camp and saw the tanner toss a bag into the small cart and make for his hobbled mule. "I see no children here."

"Then humor me, man, and make a choice: would you follow him or me?"

"You already know my choice," he spat as he heard the squeak of wooden wheels and turned his back on the shadow before him. Not far beyond speaking distance, the cart picked up speed and Arach heard the tanner's string of curses under muted breath.

But then the words were drowned and swallowed by the deafening lurch of wounded earth. Beneath his feet, the ground vanished, reappeared, and split into halves, thirds; a chasm descending into unknown darkened depths. Within the space he fell, a painful tumble down a canyon of ever-shifting stone, dirt, grass, and debris. At last, and with a sudden painful thud, he reached its floor - a wide stone surface at the foot of crumbling rock walls - and stared into the darkness of deep, starless night overhead. He took a breath, winced, and felt himself over for any signs of broken bones or serious injuries. None were found.

Cautiously, he rolled over onto bruised and scraped hands and knees, waiting for the final shower of falling stones to hit the earth around him with a chorus of sharp, staccato cracks. He crawled, moved, and pulled himself forward to the vertical wall he'd tumbled down moments before, touching its rough rocky face. "Rimmel!" he shouted, the echo of his voice the only answer. Once more he cried and pounded fist against the wall, an act that prompted one more shower of falling stones upon his unsuspecting bare head.

Alone, exhausted, and utterly spent, Arach succumbed to the gentle voice inside, lay his body down, and slept.

*

Dawn arrived at long last, its softness a comforting blanket above him. The traveler opened his eyes, no time to laze the morning away, and stripped the cavalcade of colors out of sight and mind. Reality was now before him, a pair of sheer towering walls to left and right, and he drew in a helpless breath at the sight of them. He sat up, ignored the growl in his stomach, and studied the wide and dreadfully long chasm that had swallowed him whole. "Well, then," he muttered to no one in particular and stood to his feet, "I suppose there's only one thing to be done." He scratched his unkempt beard and took the first step forward.

"Hello?" he called with both hands wrapped around his mouth, waiting as the word bounced back to him thrice. Eyes closed, he paused, listening for something - anything - to fill his ringing ears. *Nothing*. He resumed his slow but steady pace, gazing from left to right along the canyon floor and up beyond the distant out of reach ledge.

Ahead, the path doglegged to the left, the way beyond impossible to see. He zigzagged around a fallen boulder, then another; noted how lush patches of grass covered one side of each massive earthen clod. Arach reached out, brushing his hand against the soft green cushion ripped callously from its home above. He clutched at a handful of the cool green blades, tugged them out of the displaced boulder, and left the roots clinging for life in the dirt. A breeze entered the chasm and he opened his palm, watching as the grass twirled playfully toward another fallen mammoth from above and landed softly on a splintered plank of rough, shattered wood.

His hand fell, the grass ignored, and he glimpsed a pile of tattered animal skins strewn about the canyon floor. He ran for them, followed their imprecise trail, and was led to the far side of the boulder nearest the western wall to his right. Four twisted hooves came into view and a stab of pity weighed him down. The air around him thickened as he looked into a pair of wide, frightened animal eyes still open in death. Arach thought of his own horse, wondered where he was in the chaos, and swallowed the pang of fear for the helpless, abandoned animal. He wiped a pair of sweaty palms against his sides and followed the twisted harness to the shattered, lopsided cart. Eyes focused on the brutal wreckage, the traveler failed to see the carnage at his feet and stepped in a sticky pool of thick, congealing blood. He gave a start, finding the pair of fur-covered trousers he'd expected to find all along. They were the only part of the tanner he could see from that angle, the rest of the body hidden beneath the fractured cart. "Rimmel?" he called as he navigated the perimeter of the wagon as best he could. "Rimmel, can you hear me? It's Arach, the traveler."

A weak, unsteady moan gave answer as the peaceful morning breeze breathed another sigh into the air. Arach stumbled painfully across stone, blood, and wood but reached the rear of the cart and gazed down upon the man trapped beneath it. The fallen boulder of earth and stone rested precariously close to the tanner's head, a portion of it crushing the back and saddle of the fallen mule. Arach took the horrid view in, wondering how he - all by his lonesome - could save the tanner from a slow, painful death. "Can you move, my friend?" he asked, voice serene as the dawn sky above.

The tanner turned his head to the side, looking Arach in the face. "My fingers-" Rimmel rasped before erupting into a bout of painful coughs followed by a chilling liquid wheeze and gasp.

Arach leaned forward, careful not to shift his weight upon the cart. He placed a gentle hand on the man's forehead, wiping the sweat from the cold, clammy brow. "Peace now, my friend. Forgive me for making you speak." He looked down, noticed the blood around the tanner's abdomen for the first time. "Can you feel your legs, Rimmel? Blink twice if you can." He waited hopefully for the response, a pair of blinks that never came. Arach nodded, licking his lips. "Okay, then. Well," the traveler began and swatted aside a wave of uncertainty threatening to flood his peace from within. "I'm going to get you out of here. I will unstrap the mule first and see if I can push the wagon aside. It may cause a bit of a mess," he said and wiped a thick trail of mucus from the man's mouth, "and we may lose some of your animal skins in the process...but I will salvage what I can of your winter stock. Fair enough?"

He soaked in the feeble smile, praying it wouldn't be the tanner's last. Carefully, he stepped around the cart, through liters of blood, and across a vicious pile of knife-like slivers of wood. He unstrapped half of the harness from the mule, realizing the other half wouldn't budge with the weight of the beast resting heavily upon it. His eyes fell to the clutter and chaos around the cart, finding exactly what was needed. Arach grabbed the long, serrated knife, placed it against the leather strap nearest to where it attached to the cart, and sawed back and forth through painfully gritted teeth. He ignored the pain in his shoulder, arm, and hand, letting out a cry of absolute joy as the leather snapped and wagon weight shifted as the mule detached from the crippling cart.

"Are you still with me?" Arach asked as he made his way back to the rear of the cart and placed the knife upon the ground. A single nod greeted him as he looked down at the pale-faced tanner. He gripped the fractured wagon in his hands, ignored the biting sting of splinters digging deep into his hands, and strained with all his might. The cart failed to budge. He tried again in vain, the pain unreal as the wagon remained steadfastly in place and failed to move so much as a single hopeful inch. "Hold on, my friend. We can do this," Arach grunted and resumed the gut-wrenching process of a third fruitless attempt to save the tanner's quickly depleting life. He shifted positions and failed twice more. Arms and muscles numb beyond all use, he sank to the ground and rested his head upon the splintered cart in unequivocal defeat.

The raspy moan reached his ears once more and he inhaled a calm, steadying breath. He replaced the look of a man defeated with a mask of confidence, wondering if the tanner could see straight through it. Arach crossed the distance to the trapped man, knelt at his head, and gave the tanner a reassuring grip of the shoulder. "We'll get you out of here soon enough, Rimmel. Another moment is all I need."

A hopeless pair of eyes fell to the knife, returning themselves to the traveler's own. An almost imperceptible nod - such a hopeless, voiceless last request - preceded another brutal cough much worse than all that came before it. Arach wiped the blood from Rimmel's mouth, letting the tears of despair and failure fall from his own misty eyes. "Do not ask that of me, my friend," he whispered and pushed himself back upon his feet. Gently, he placed a trembling hand upon the wagon, wiping his face with the other. "I can do this."

"You cannot," came the voice - that dreaded, hated voice - and Arach jerked around in unexpected fear. "But I can."

Chapter Thirteen

Tiro dismissed the repeated offers for help, approached the towering tree, and removed the forest green hood from his sweat-laden head. Up his gaze went, all the way up to treetops piercing clouds in a bright blue sky. The bowman smiled, knowing he was at home here. He inserted powerful fingers into the clefts of rough grey bark and began the comfortable ascent into the heavens.

"Are you sure about this?" Cephan asked just loud enough for the scurrying hunter to hear.

He pressed the ball of his left foot into the trunk, pulled himself up with a vise-like grip, and set his right foot in the perfect place. With a speed that surprised all six of the huddled men upon the ground, he pulled himself up the tree and to the first landing of smooth, thick branches stretched out toward its nearby leaf-covered friends. He peered down from the perch with a sly grin, making time to salute the red-haired rebel commander who was wearing a look of terror across his face.

Tiro returned his focus to the task at hand, studying the next portion of the aerial climb. As before, his hands found themselves digging into ancient cracks and shallow crevices etched into the thick towering tree. Up he climbed, not content to stop halfway; further and further he went to the dismay of the soldiers crouching fearfully below. He climbed as far as possible until there was nowhere left to go and nothing more to bear his lithe youthful weight.

Steadily, patiently, he tested two supple branches extending outward from the now narrow trunk - first his left foot, then his right - and was confident they would hold. With his left arm, he hugged the trunk; with his right, he cautiously lifted a wispy leaf-covered branch obstructing his view from a clearing beside a road in the near distance. Tiro squinted, twisted uncomfortably from his hiding place in the heights, and pulled aside another branch that blocked his narrow view. "Not good enough," he muttered and allowed himself to slide six feet down the trunk to another landing. Muffled curses carried upward to his ears, all his fellow soldiers scrambling to catch the falling boy. He stifled a laugh, stuck his head out far enough to be seen from below, and mouthed the words *I'm fine!*

Furious and on the verge of a nervous breakdown, Cephan jabbed an accusatory finger Tiro's way and motioned for him to come down "At once!"

From above, the hunter paused in thoughtful consideration, recalling the captain's precise words to the westerner below: *"Give him a measure of freedom; see where it takes him."* Tiro smiled, pressed himself into the tree, and found his footing on a thick north-facing branch suspended forty feet in the air. His eyes traced a line from his feet, all the way across the empty chasm, and up the adjacent trunk of the nearest tree. The view from over there seemed much less obstructed by leaves and limbs than the one he claimed at the moment. *Okay then.* Tiro breathed through his nose. He touched each dark green finger of the symbol stretched across his expanding chest, letting the air fill his lungs. *Let's see where my freedom takes me.*

The thrill of flight overtook him, propelling him outward and slightly down. Across the chasm he soared, the rustling of vivid green branches behind, the hissing of frightened obscenities rising from the earth below. Enraptured, he opened his arms, stretched out for the rapidly approaching trunk. His foot found the thick sturdy limb of the neighboring tree, his hands the rough grey trunk. Pulse racing, Tiro lifted wide, glimmering eyes to the far realm of blue beyond, the thrill of cheating death a rare, enlivening pleasure.

"Tiro!" the boy heard from far below, the tone in the voice far from enlivened or pleased. "Tiro!" it called again, louder and closer than before. "Don't make me hurl a spear up there, boy! Get down here now!"

He held a weightless hand out to the infuriated commander below and noticed his neck, cheeks, and forehead closely matched his fire-red hair. *Wait,* he mouthed before adding *please* as an afterthought. The boy turned his attention back upon the heights, any protest Cephan could give successfully avoided.

Up Tiro went, the constant tug of gravity no detriment to his progress, until he felt the unsettling sway of a narrowing trunk on the verge of splitting fast asunder. He found his balance, directing his sight to the grassy clearing a quarter-mile distant. The hunter's heart plummeted straight back to earth at the sight of a horse-drawn wagon parked beside the road. "Tara," he whispered, his soul extended in multiple frantic tendrils, their quivering, desperate tips reaching out for any connection to give a singular shred of peace. He found none.

He blocked the wagon and its unknown contents from his mind, focusing instead on what he could see without question. *One...two, three...four,* he counted patiently, all the way up to the number eighteen. Once more the boy counted, knowing full well the devastation that could be caused from rushing the basics. Straight down the grey shaft his vision turned again, to the huddled cluster of men below and the livid yet curious eyes buried deep within the mass of red hair. *Eighteen,* he mouthed and held his left palm out and parallel to the forest floor below; open, close, open, close, open, close, three fingers extended. Cephan nodded, correctly repeating the numerical symbol from his shadowy spot below. Tiro gave a thumbs-up sign and waited for further instructions.

After a brief consultation between earth-bound rebels, Tiro was waved down from his perch above. "Well?" he asked as he let go of the final branch, hit the ground with a crouch, and stood to his feet amongst the men.

The slow shake of the commander's head wasn't the most encouraging sign. "We're turning back. Much too risky."

"Risky?" Tiro repeated as he glanced from face to face. His attention returned to the westerner. "Since when was safety a prime concern for bloodthirsty rebel warriors?"

"Seven against eighteen, Tiro. Not worth it." The commander lifted his right hand and drew a circle of retreat in the air. "Time to return home. Maybe next time."

"There was a wagon," Tiro added, a slight tinge of desperation seeping deep into each word, "like they use to transport girls. We should do what we can."

"Tiro," Cephan began, his tone understanding, his mind completely made up. "It's best-"

"-to do our job!" he hissed to the surprise of the rebels encircling him. "To do what we all signed up for!" The hunter drew his bow from its holster and reached for the detached string at his hip.

Cephan stepped forward, placing a hand on Tiro's expanding and contracting chest. "Calm yourself. And trust me. This isn't your call, Tiro, it's mine."

"Then go ahead. Tell the captain I got lost." He continued stringing the bow and pulled the dark hood over his head. "I have the forest. I have the advantage." Tiro opened the top flap of his quiver, counting twenty-five arrows. *More than enough.* "You can join me, watch from safety, or return to camp. Your choice."

He turned on his heel and left the circle of six to discuss their own fate.

"Tiro!" Cephan cried as softly as possible after a moment's pause. The boy stopped and glanced back toward the commander with dark eyes of unshakable determination. "Do you at least have a plan?"

The hunter nodded. "Follow me. I will not fail you."

*

He was a ghost; so close he could hear their words, smell their stench. They were to his back, a thick tree his last and only protection from a painful, brutal death. Tiro glanced right, saw the other bowman in his squad of six, and nodded reassuringly. He looked beyond the camouflaged rebel, saw Cephan kneeling with drawn sword, ready and barely fidgeting through the nerves. To Tiro's left was another swordsman, also armed, ready, hidden. The fifth and sixth rebels were near but out of sight, presumably armed and ready as the others.

They'd better be ready, Tiro thought to himself as he notched an arrow, standing to his feet. Slowly, he rotated around the massive trunk, found the nearest servant of the Empire, and marked the unknowing fool for a sudden, certain death. The blackened bow lifted, bending silently under the tension. Tiro drew a breath, let it out, and glanced around in panicked disbelief. Underfoot, a foreign grumble. The hunter's eyes darted for those of his fellow rebels and saw each man staring confusedly at the ground, which shifted side to side. Through a sudden twitch of earth and frantic sway of limbs, Tiro fell sidelong against the steady trunk, the groan and crash throughout the region masking any and all noise the rebels happened to make. He jumped toward the roots, steadied himself, and lifted his left arm above his head as a shield from falling branches and bark.

The quake ceased. In its place, shouts and chaos from the clearing. Tiro glanced left and right, gave another nod, and stood to his feet armed, the bitter taste of bloodlust thick inside his mouth. He loosed the first arrow and the next, watching both men fall hidden into the knee-high grass unseen. The third arrow flew, a gruesome head shot that found its helmetless victim's temple, and still the fallen remained unseen by all imperial foes.

Tiro knew the moment of truth was upon him and prayed the bowman to his left would not allow nerves or adrenaline get the best of him. He waited patiently, watching as the imperials glanced left, right, up, and down - everywhere, in fact, but toward the edge of forest partially sheltering Tiro or their comrades bleeding thick crimson rivers into the grass. Four soldiers stood together, their focus on calming two pair of bucking, frightened horses harnessed to the wagon. The hunter took another breath, stilling his hand for an opportune moment to arrive. After what seemed an eternity, a soldier stepped backwards, taking a step from the calming tethered beasts. Tiro traced his path with arrow drawn, watching him move toward his fellow comrade.

The hunter fired. His eye charted its course, a stunning arc of perfection, patience, and beauty. Quick and sharp as lightning, the arrow passed clean through the neck of the walking soldier, lodging itself into the padded shoulder of the next. Tiro drew another arrow, cursing as he saw it exit the soldier's torso and penetrate the flesh of one of the four spooked beasts.

Frantic eyes darted to the shadowed line of trees, eventually finding the bowman at its edge. Harmless imperial fingers pointed like spears and jumbled orders resounded as weapons were drawn in a desperate attempt to end the life of the cloaked intruder. Tiro drew one more arrow, a parting shot intended to provoke them even further, and watched a puff of blood spew and vanish from behind the collapsing soldier.

From his left, he saw the other bowman depart the line of trees, aim, and let his own barbed arrow fly. Lost in the moment, Tiro whooped in joy and excitement, watching the feathered missile hit its unsuspecting target from behind. Within seconds, another fell, the pile of dead and dying now seven with one more helplessly injured. He paused for breath and saw the remaining enemy soldiers predictably split their forces - five to the northern bowman, five his direction. *Nearly there,* he encouraged himself as he bolted to the right, welcomed the sheltering eaves above him, and fled noisily into the woods. Straight past the first hidden swordsmen he ran and the second shortly thereafter, who gave him a wink and a nod respectively.

The hunter found his mark, a tree next to a shallow dip in the earth, and spun at its lip. The tumult of shouts and hurried footfalls entered the forest and he stepped into sight from behind his chosen trunk. Tiro heard their curses, felt their hatred, and let it fill his ears with delight. He raised his bow, a feint which prompted all five heavily armored soldiers to halt their progress to cower behind what safety they could find. He leapt into the shallow hiding place, fell to his face with bow still in hand, and crawled north on his stomach through the dry, leaf-covered gully.

Terror filled his ears, a joyous sound, and Tiro lifted his hooded head above the lip of his hiding place. A red fountain erupted in the dim afternoon light, the thud of helmeted head hitting earth filling his ears. "Well done," he whispered to the dual swordsmen who appeared from nowhere to surprise the unsuspecting charge of imperial soldiers. Tiro stood, strafed to the left to afford himself a worthy shot, and released his arrow. It took the enemy off guard from the side, drawing his attention from the rebel poised to hack his arm off at the elbow. The bowman moved past roots and trunks, fired another lethal shot, and watched in admiration as his fellow swordsmen finished off the last of the enemy with a powerful downstroke through the collarbone.

The swordsman kicked the bloody body to the earth with a yelp and turned his fierce eyes to the young rebel approaching with his bow. "Victory!"

"Not yet," Tiro answered and waved both men to follow him north through the woods.

They ran, unafraid of the noise they made and slowed their pace at the sight of blood-covered trees, headless bodies, and Cephan lifting a sweating canteen of water to his lips. The second bowman nursed a small wound in his arm, smirking as Tiro and the two swordsmen approached with admirable looks toward the carnage littering the forest floor.

"Well, then," the red-haired commander said as

he returned the canteen to his hip. "Took you boys long enough." He eyed the panting bowman, nodded with a smirk, and added, "But I would call that a smashing success."

Chapter Fourteen

"You!" Arach seethed in open hatred. "Get away from here!"

Clothed in royal white, a false look of pain and anguish across its face, the wraith ignored the heated words and stretched out for the pale, dying tanner. "My child," it sobbed, crystal tears falling visibly upon the blood-smeared floor, "you are hurt. Let me heal your wounds and lift your troubled soul."

"Ignore him, Rimmel," Arach flared through clenched teeth and sheltered the trapped man from the being's sight. "He is no angel of light, but a liar and deceiver." The traveler glared behind himself to the approaching apparition. "He means you harm."

An angel? the tanner mouthed in silence and twitched, blinked his eyes in rapid, uncontrollable desperation. *Please,* he begged, his teeth, tongue, and lips coated in a thick layer of regurgitated blood. *Help me!*

Tears and sweat comingled, falling from Arach's cheeks upon the man beneath him. Each drop found an encrusted, bloody target, transformed each region into a pink liquid stream that trickled down the tanner's face and into the dirt below. He began to shiver, feeling the nearness of the wraith not far behind and reconsidered the cold, sharp blade still within an arm's reach.

"Your poor beast," the crowned being murmured as it approached the downed wagon. Arach glared, feeling the insatiable lust for blood and life seep from the translucent being. "He was a faithful servant in life, was he not?" The answer was revealed in mournful, failing eyes. "He is now in a better place and anxiously awaits you. But your time does not have to come just yet."

A weight visibly lifted from Rimmel's battered face and he strained to see beyond the traveler blocking his sight. "No," Arach stared down at the man, shaking his head with the word, "do not listen to him!"

The creak and crack of shifting, splitting wood echoed furiously around the chasm, Arach lifted his lowered head in time to see the cart smash into a thousand pieces against the furthest wall. The boulder shifted next, rolling a short distance away, and crumbled into a cloud of dust and roots and stones. Unobstructed, the wraith moved forward, touching the pair of bloody legs broken far beyond repair. It lifted eyes of sorrow to the tanner, opening its mouth to speak. "My child, I feel your pain. Your wounds are grave, no fault of your own-"

"Leave this place at once, wraith."

"-but perhaps I can help." It leaned forward, stretched out a quivering transparent hand to the now-peaceful face of the tanner, and wiped a smear of blood from the man's neck.

"Do not listen to him, Rimmel. You must trust me now. I'm begging you."

"Do you want to be healed, child? To walk, to run? To follow me up and out of this place?" It motioned to the canyon surrounding them. "Can I help you? Do you trust me?"

A sigh, a pure, deep breath, and a hopeful nod. "Yes," he moaned, unafraid of pain. "I do."

"For you are wise, unlike some." It nodded. From its chest, a slow, thick drip of the black oozing substance fell to the earth with an acidic hiss. "But the wise know nothing in life can ever be given for free. Especially what is given in second life."

Rimmel struggled for breath, wheezed, and

spoke through a chilling gurgling sound. "Please...I want to live."

"And you shall, child." With an anxious twitch, the wraith reached out, panted uncontrollably, and covered the eyes of the paralyzed tanner. "But you will lose these...and follow me."

Arach stared in horror as two thin trails of floating milky substance exited the eyes of the tanner and vanished within its pale, translucent hand. "You monster!" he spat and lunged for the solitary blade, imagining raising the knife and aiming for the naked human neck that gasped for breath and life in fear. *It is the humane thing to do*, he thought and waited for his inner self to confirm the cruel but just use of logic. The voice was silent and still, and Arach let a sob of guilt stay his hand, if only for a moment.

The mass-less being reached out, clamping his indecisive hand with its own. Before his eyes, the figure transformed from light to darkness, its haunting grey orbs boring shades of hate and malice into his soul. The hand that gripped his straining arm, now a slimy, snake-like tendril, shook the blade from aching fingers with a noisy clatter. "And you think I am the monster, Arach?"

"I-" he began before trailing off in shame.

"*-was only trying to help*, yes? Is that what you would have us believe? And how often have you *tried to help* and only failed, man?"

Blind and shaken, the tanner's eyes flitted about in pain and abject confusion.

"Rimmel-"

"Silence, foul traitor!" the wraith hissed, growing in stature and size. "Bow before me and observe." It lashed out, struck the traveler in the chest, and laughed as Arach fell immobile to the canyon floor. Its attention returned to the blind, dazed tanner. "My child," it began softly as it hovered above the broken frame of a man, "you will soon feel cold. But you must trust me. I am now your eyes, your guide, your compass. I am light and all knowing. I will not lead you astray." The tendril lifted with a nervous twitch, traveled across the body of the bleeding man, and stopped above the parted lips that gasped for air. The shadow turned, gazing upon the paralyzed traveler with delight.

"Please," Arach began, the invisible burden upon his chest a weight restricting breath and speech, "I'm begging."

With grey, haunting orbs fixed firmly upon the traveler, the wraith forced its tendril into the agape mouth panting for one more breath, one more chance at life. Down it traveled - through lungs and heart, past veins and arteries - until at last its slow internal course came to a halt and the tendril moved no more. "Now breathe, my child," it commanded the prone, filled man.

Arach watched the thick oily substance depart the wraith in a steady oozing stream and fill the quickly dying tanner. The darkness churned and flowed beneath his skin, transposing the flesh from sunburned pale to sickly grey. Rimmel's blind eyes clouded over, the dual irises that danced in shades of speckled green now nothing more than lifeless smears of white. His chest ballooned above a new pair of lungs and Rimmel exhaled into the tendril buried like a root within his core. With the single powerful breath, the grisly pools of blood receded like a tide as the gaping chasm in the tanner's wounded abdomen sealed shut with a spine-tingling slurping sound. Out of the man and into the tendril the blood and gore flowed, where it entered the hovering wraith with rapture. Speechless, Arach stared, letting the tremors of horror depart his convoluted soul as ripples into the cold, merciless world around him.

The wraith withdrew the engorged tendril, allowing the last remaining drops of blood weep upon the canyon floor. It looked upon Arach and flung the bloody remnants upon him in streaks of warm, oozing strands. "Arise, my child, for today, you have been healed," it hissed, its cold, dull eyes a pair of daggers aimed not at the tanner, but the traveler streaked in crimson.

The tanner shifted, placing both hands upon the rocky ground. The legs moved next - those same broken and lifeless legs mere moments before - and pushed the blind man up and onto steady, unwavering feet. Rimmel reached out, waved both trembling hands before his dead milky eyes, and touched his heaving chest. "Am I...am I dead? Is anyone there? Can anyone hear me?"

Arach saw the evil mouth split into its own self-satisfied chasm before the wraith turned its attention from him to the blind newborn of a man. "You are alive, my child; more alive than you have ever been before."

"But I cannot see." He turned toward the voice, took a timid, cautious step, and then another. "There was a man with me - my friend. Where is he?"

Arach opened his mouth, closed it again, and took a pained, uncertain breath. "I am here, Rimmel. How do you feel?"

The clouded eyes blinked, a shade of thought or sadness passed from one into the other. "I'm cold...and thirsty." He brought a claw-like hand to his face and patted the mass of hair upon his head. "I'm afraid, Arach."

The traveler scowled in hatred at the lightless figure and winced. "Then we are two companions in the very same boat, my friend." The weight upon his chest dissipated and he stood to his feet, wiped the disgusting streaks of blood from his face, and ignored the being who watched in silent glee. Rimmel took a tentative step toward his voice. "Don't move just yet; I'm coming to you. I'll lend you my arm." Arach spanned the distance in a dozen or so steps, reached out to the shivering tanner, and lifted the canteen at his hip. He shook it and knew by its sound that the canteen was no more than a quarter full. "There isn't much, perhaps three good sips." He pressed the small opening to his friend's mouth. "But take what you need and we'll search for more."

Fire scorched the tanner's tongue. Rimmel lifted clawed hands to his throat, bending at the waist as he gagged and writhed in pain. The leather canteen fell with a clatter to the dry, cracked earth and spilled what little contents remained into the dirt at the traveler's feet. Rimmel lashed out in pain and anger, tripped on a stone, and fell to the chasm floor with a painful thud. "Why?" he managed between a hailstorm of debilitating coughs as he struggled for relief and untainted air. "Why are you so heartless? So evil?"

Laughter filled his ears, the chilling trill of wretched despair, and the wraith floated past Arach toward the blind man hacking on hands and knees. "How true your words, child," it hissed and came to a halt beside Rimmel. "But I am here, and where I am, no harm shall befall you." The tendril stretched out, wrapped itself around the blind man's wrist, and led the open palm toward the oozing liquid seeping from the darkened being's chest. Covered in the tar-like filth, the tanner's hand dropped as the wraith released its grip. "Drink, my child, and quench your thirst."

"Rimmel," Arach stammered before being silenced by an icy look. He followed the path of the rising hand, watching as the fingers touched a pair of dry, cracked lips, and traced the slow visible trail all the way down the throat of the blinded tanner.

Rimmel's head lifted, the hazy eyes pleading and searching for the wraith as a lost child seeks his mother.

"More?"

A nod, as hands reached out in desperation for the center of darkness. The pair were covered from fingertips to wrist and lifted once again to quivering, receptive lips.

"Your strength, my child? Has it returned to you?"

Another nod. "Yes, master."

"And are you ready to leave this place and follow me? Are you ready to leave your past behind? To become great?"

"I am," Rimmel answered, turning his sightless eyes eerily close to the spot where Arach stood and watched in mute fascination. "But what of the foreigner? What will become of him?"

The wraith approached the silent watcher, withdrew its tendril, and poised it mid-air. "What do you think, my child? What should become of the man who tried to harm you?"

A pause preceded a spiteful, inhuman sneer. "Let me kill him, master. As an offering to you for restoring my life and loving me as I am."

His heart skipped a beat, and Arach looked from one foul thing to the other. He searched for the fallen knife, wondering if the weapon was as worthless against the servant as it was the master.

"No," the wraith answered. The inky tendril returned to the tanner and attached itself to the base of Rimmel's neck. "We will leave our friend to his own devices. Let him stumble about of his own accord, see how far it takes him." The two moved forward - Rimmel in front, the wraith close behind - and came to a halt at the sheer face of the imposing eastern wall. The quake was brief, but strong enough to crack and split a narrow opening into the foot of the cliff.

Into the yawning mouth of the cave entrance the two stepped as Arach watched from his place beside the crushed, lifeless mule. The wraith turned, waiting for the traveler to speak.

"I'm not coming."

"I shall leave the way open for you," it spoke and stepped further into the darkness of the tunnel. "For I still have hope for you, my child."

"I'm not your child!" He spat upon the ground, withholding the dire curse he wanted so desperately to hurl in place of the useless knife. "And I will never need your help, wraith!"

"So you say, human."

The shadow vanished within the darkness, its accursed whispers of endearment to its new slave all the encouragement Arach needed to escape. He retrieved the empty canteen and fallen knife, turned his back upon the passage, and set his eyes for south.

CHAPTER FIFTEEN

"Commander Cephan tells me you have some difficulty following orders."

Tiro swallowed, his throat parched as an arid wasteland, and considered his words carefully. He could feel the captain's intense frigid glare and focused his attention on the green palm stretched across the man's chest. "I know my strengths, sir, and do not doubt them. Each step I make is calculated and considered."

"And what of every leap?"

He felt a twitch at the back of his neck, refusing to acknowledge it. "Surely he gave you more feedback, sir."

Hemas drummed the cluttered desk with the fingers of his right hand and studied the nervous boy before him. After giving the desk a final tap, he opened his mouth again. "Surely."

Tiro fidgeted subconsciously, shifting his weight from left to right foot. "May I hear it? I would like to know his thoughts, Captain."

"Do you?" He waited for the nod and the boy to lift his nervous eyes. "Well, where should I begin?" The captain looked down at a yellowing piece of rolled parchment, smoothed its edges out, and placed a pair of knives along the top and bottom edges.

As inconspicuously as was possible, Tiro shifted to the aching balls of his feet and craned his neck to catch an upside down glimpse of the report. He winced. The whole page was riddled with illegibly scribbled notes, many of the words underlined three times for added emphasis.

"Commander Cephan seems to imply you found sport in the art of causing him premature heart failure."

"I was only trying to-"

"If your commanding officer orders you to climb a tree, you climb a tree. If he tells you to climb down, you climb down. No waiting, no dragging of the feet, no abrupt change of plans." He lifted his gaze from the parchment to the boy who stood at ease before him. "It really is quite simple, Tiro."

"I was-"

"This is not a one-man show, soldier. This is an

army." Hemas leaned forward, tracing his fingers to the corners of the desk and back again. "We are under-strength, under-supplied, and very often overwhelmed. We cannot afford so much as one unnecessary death or foolish injury. Especially from an easy-to-prevent accident. A broken branch, a misplaced foot, a hasty order...things of this nature can upset the entire course of our plans, Tiro."

He clenched his jaw and held his tongue.

"Are we on the same page, soldier? Please tell me we are."

Tiro lifted his eyes and stood to attention. "Yes sir."

"Good. Then make sure it doesn't happen again." The parchment demanding his attention once again, Hemas dropped his eyes to the black words scribbled lengthwise across it. "When you made the unplanned decision to leave your comrades and make for the clearing on your own, what was your main concern? The eighteen imperial troops or the empty transport wagon?"

Deflated, Tiro felt himself tense once more. "I didn't know the wagon was empty, sir."

"You didn't answer my question: troops or wagon?"

He knew what Hemas was thinking, knew his answer was unavoidable. "You know my heartfelt goal is to rid the earth of each and every man who bears the mark of the Empire. It consumes me, sir. It's why I'm here." Emotionless eyes stared back at him, his words mere pebbles tossed against the skin of an unconcerned behemoth. He continued. "As far as the wagon," he paused to collect his thoughts and wiped the sweat from his uncovered brow, "I knew she was not there. Even from my perch in the tree, I could sense it and knew it as fact. But if I can help another's sister, daughter..."

Hemas waited for the boy to finish his thoughts, a collection of words that never came. "When I first met you, Tiro, I found you cold and heartless. How wrong I was." He removed the paperweights, letting the parchment snap back to a tubular shape of its own accord. "You have a unique compassion for others in need. But you also have a duty to your brothers, Tiro. Do you want to bear the cruel burden of needless, preventable deaths on your own shoulders? Those men who fight by your side need you. Each of them is a husband, son, and brother of someone outside of these walls who cares very deeply for them."

"You're right," the hunter agreed, "but we have chosen to protect and defend the weak, correct?"

The captain pondered the question, letting the corners of his mouth raise ever so slightly. "I'm the one asking the questions, soldier. Think on your mistakes, Tiro. Learn from them. Otherwise, job well done. You impressed the commander for the most part, which impresses me in turn. Now go get some sleep. We have much to discuss tomorrow morning. You're dismissed."

Tiro nodded, held the sigh of relief within until the tent was far behind him, and allowed a smile to crease his anxious, trembling lips.

*

The furious clang of bells jolted him awake, the smiling apparition of his sister fading like mist. He opened his eyes to a lonely shade of darkness and clutched the corners of his blanketed cot. "To your stations!" echoed in his mind as he rubbed sleep and sadness from his throbbing head. *What stations?* Tiro thought as he sat upright on his pallet to let his confused mind and sight adjust to bleak surroundings. He sighed, ignoring the frenzy of chaos and confusion beyond the rough canvas walls, and mentally reached out for the beaming girl who had been right there mere moments ago. *Come back, Tara. I need you.*

"To your stations, men! On the double!"

As if suddenly slapped awake, the hoarsely shouted words from beyond his sight had a curious effect on the creeping fog that clouded

Tiro's mind and eyes. As the pounding blood rushed to his head, Tiro's vision adjusted to the empty dark square of a room. He jumped to his bare feet with a muted curse for himself and his foolish moment of weakness. *Don't let the dream world govern you,* the boy commanded himself as he ripped the tent flap aside and stepped into a scene of clearly defined order amid carefully controlled panic. Out of tents they poured, sleep-deprived men suddenly wakened and ready for whatever course of action greeted them in the deep of night. Tiro fought off a wave of embarrassment once he realized he was the only soldier affixed to the door of his tent with no weapon, no plan to move, and a mask of disorientation across his face. He leapt back into his tent, reached for the bow and quiver laid carefully on the ground, and fell to hands and knees in a frustrating attempt to locate his missing pair of boots.

Frantic bells resounded again, the metallic clang of terror, and the hunter muttered to himself as he reached under the cot to retrieve his pair of black knee-high boots. *Focus, Tiro,* he urged himself as he wrapped his hooded cloak across his frame and exited the tent with bow in one hand, quiver in the other. "Where to?" he called out to a fellow bowman who either ignored the question or failed to even hear the words above the raucous din. Tiro traced his steps, following as close behind the archer as the rushing waves of men allowed.

An arc of rising light claimed his attention, followed by another. From the forest they came, fiery trails of orange heat all landing with sparks in the middle of camp. Some sliced through tents and erupted into bursts of white-hot fire. Others penetrated the ground, their flames erased by puffs of dying smoke. Tiro watched as one caught the arm of a running soldier, winced empathetically for the unlucky rebel, and prayed the man would drop to the earth and roll the flames out. He had no time to help or learn the rebel's fate as he followed the winding path of the sprinting bowman through camp.

Under the glimmer of arrow-fall, he found the northern camp wall and ran for the nearest ladder leading to the narrow sentry walkway above. "Move!" a shapeless voice cried from above. The boy slung his bow across his shoulder, tied the quiver around his waist, and climbed as quickly as the shaky unstable ladder allowed. "To the left, *Ghost*!" the shapeless voice called out again, and Tiro obeyed without falter.

He removed the bow from his shoulder and slunk toward the edge with head lowered and eyes raised. All along the wall were cloaked bowmen busily aiming, shooting, and reaching for their next arrow. A handful of young boys ran along the wall, their only job to drop fresh quivers at the feet of preoccupied rebels. It was a task that seemed to go unnoticed and unappreciated during the cacophony, most especially when one fell hard from the walkway with an enemy arrow lodged deep within his unprotected skull. The dull *thunk* of arrow on wood filled Tiro's ears to left and right, all along the outer wall it seemed, and Tiro returned to the inglorious task at hand. He found a wide enough hole between fellow archers to make his own stand, dropping the quiver at his scuffling feet.

Far beyond the first line of trees, he saw pockets of controlled flames scattered here and there, watching as armor-clad imperial bowmen dipped tar-covered arrows into the monstrous glow. Highlighted by the darkness, he observed the flaming arrows bob up and down through the forest until they halted, aimed for the rebel camp, and soared up into the black night sky. He drew his own bowstring to his cheek, ready as ever to unleash his own form of havoc, and aimed for his first target below.

"You're the new recruit? *The Ghost?*" the soldier to his right yelled and let his own missile fly.

Attention diverted, Tiro glanced to his side. "I am."

"Just be mindful of the fires and pitch. We don't want to find ourselves trapped in a burning forest, do we?"

Tiro considered the words, allowed the imperial bowman he had targeted to loose his own vicious arrow, and aimed for the man's visible chest. He saw the body fall and reached for another arrow.

"Keep it up, just like that," the bowman to his right said. "Give it another minute or so and we'll open the gates to release our foot soldiers and cavalry upon the fools. Just be sure to mind the friendly fire when that happens."

He nodded, spotting a soldier dipping an arrow into what appeared to be a vat of tar. It would be a difficult shot through multiple overhanging limbs, one he would not normally waste an arrow on. Tiro thought of the boy who fell delivering arrows, hating for a death such as his to be in vain. He aimed for the man's upper back, loosed the arrow, and saw the bowman stumble forward with the impact. Tiro held his breath, watching the soldier fall headlong into the bubbling pitch with a spine-tingling inhuman squeal. Tar spilled out upon the man and forest floor; uproarious laughter broke the tension up and down the rebel line, and outbursts of victorious cheers preceded another massive onslaught of flying rebel arrows. It was glorious, intoxicating, and Tiro threw his own joyous voice into the fray.

The men along the walls kept the same frenetic pace until a shout and rumble of wall and earth resounded from the left. "That will be them," the bowman to Tiro's right confirmed and both men loosed their arrows as if from a single conscious thought. "One or two more volleys and then we stand down. Make each shot count."

Both had time for one more shot and Tiro watched in fascination as the invaders dissipated in all directions to flee into the cover of dark, dense forest. "Sounds like this is nothing more than routine for you," he said through labored breath. He dropped the bow to his side and placed a hand on the ledge of the stomach-high wooden wall. "Does this happen every night?"

"Not quite." The bowman chuckled and turned his back to the trees where rebel soldiers poured into and through. He looked down, studied the interior of the camp, and nodded, the damage seemingly under control and minimal. "But some would say it happens much too often, so *routine* is probably a good enough word for it."

Tiro looked down the line of men on the wall and saw nearly all had their backs to the forest. Although it made him more than slightly uncomfortable, he turned his back like the rest and followed the archer's gaze to the camp below. "How did they find us?"

"It's all part of the routine, I suppose. We move camp, stick around a bit too long, and suffer through a night attack like this as soon as their scouts find our whereabouts and report back." He waved for Tiro to follow him along the walkway and back down the nearest ladder. "You can usually mark your calendar by this very accurate time table. Therefore, you're really quite fortunate - you can start your calendar anew in the morning without having it disrupted halfway through. And another thing you can count on is we'll be breaking camp first thing tomorrow. Time to move on to safer pastures."

"I see," Tiro replied, the distant clash of metal on metal ringing in his ears. He held the ladder for the descending bowman and took his own turn as another held the rickety bamboo poles for him.

"I'm Sy-i, by the way." The bowman threw back his hood, held out a gloved palm, and shook hands with the younger marksman. Tiro looked into his face, noticing the man's right eye was blind. Surrounding the edge of the dead, unseeing eye was a red oval of deep scar tissue.

"Tiro."

"Tiro, then. Good. Everyone around here knows your other name, but Tiro sounds more -

well - human." Sy-i smiled through a quick nod of the head. "Anyway, that was some nice shooting, Tiro. Especially for a newcomer."

He thanked the older bowman and followed him through the center of camp. "Not my first tussle with the Empire."

"Let's pray it won't be your last." Sy-i halted in the midst of a rapidly forming square of bowmen and looked Tiro up and down. "Have you been assigned to a squad yet?"

The hunter shook his head, uncertainty prompting him to tense up and fear for his place among the large rebel force. "Not yet."

"Perhaps tomorrow, then." He began to vanish within the group of bowmen and stuck his head out for a few parting words: "By the way - you did wonderful, *Ghost*. Did he not, men?"

A chorus of affirmative responses lifted his spirits, but only just enough to remind him of his loneliness. He thought of Marik, wishing he had a friend to confide in. He took a step backward, the first uncertain step in a path with no clear destination that night, and vanished from sight and sound.

Chapter Sixteen

The melodious refrain reached his ears, giving him pause. *You're hearing things,* the inner voice exclaimed, choking his optimism with a stubborn fist. Arach resumed his uniform pace to the south, felt his tongue swell uncomfortably in his dry, thirsty mouth, and swallowed through the raw pain. He stopped once again, lifted closed eyes to the cloudy sky above, and listened for the faint percussive notes of water upon stone. "I know I heard something," he muttered aloud to himself and the silent lifeless stones around him. "I can't be going crazy."

Are you sure? the pessimistic voice responded, its gloomy tone a distraction much too weighty for the lonely, thirsty man.

The traveler shook his head to dislodge the negative thoughts. He had been trudging along for hours without a bite of food or water, had all but given up the dim flicker of hope for finding anything substantial that day. No sign of life - or even death - had passed him by since the haunting morning confrontation. To make matters worse, the unwelcome, disruptive voice within had repeatedly questioned whether or not the abandonment of the mysterious cave was a choice he'd soon regret.

Although the chasm was far from a perfectly scored channel in the earth, its course stayed mostly true in its north to south bearing. As such, Arach knew the stream must be following his southerly course like a faithful companion on his left hand side, somewhere up the wall and far beyond his reach. He could not hear or smell it, but felt its lingering, comforting existence. Always present, always faithful, he wanted it, longed for it, needed it more than food or rest. It frustrated him more than words could express, for he knew the wraith understood these complex inward thoughts, believed the foul creature had intentionally stripped from him the two things that mattered most in life and homebound journey: his trusty horse and the life-giving stream beyond all sight and sound.

Arach looked skyward, up beyond the sheer eastern cliff, and to its distant rocky lip. He envisioned the coolness of the stream, imagined its meandering path from the northern mountains to the southern coast somewhere far before him. "You must be near," he spoke aloud to the inanimate body of water. "So close and yet so far away."

The wall drew him in, a powerful riptide pulling him nearer to itself, and the traveler stepped forward, the outstretched fingertips of his right hand leading him as a man leads a tethered beast. Thoughtlessly, Arach allowed himself to be led, placing his hand flat against the cold, hard wall of stone. He imagined the solid mass splitting open at his touch as it had for the wraith that same morning. The traveler shook the thought from his head and banished the vision from his mind. He was no wraith, no supernatural being with inhuman power to haunt, heal, or cause the grassy earth to swallow men whole. Instead, he kept the hand pressed firmly against the cool earthen stone and traced a wavering, bumpy path along its surface, hoping beyond all hope to find and touch a hidden trail of water in his relentless journey south.

Ahead, an outward curve in the canyon caused a portion of the wall to jut from view. The traveler took instant notice, his instinct perking up much like the ears of his old faithful companion's, and picked up speed with a heart full of hope and promise. The echoes of his heavy footfall reached his ears, but in those brief stretches of stillness when no foot slapped hard upon the ground, another familiar rhythm resounded. He stopped, held his breath, and heard an incessant trickle and the bell-like sound of water dripping from on high, of droplets reunited with kindred elements. The traveler's hand left its stony path; he ran as fast as aching feet could carry him.

"I knew it!" he cried as he rounded the curve, laughed with genuine glee, and gazed into the heavens. From above, the water trickled in a slow, winding descent down the face of the wall where its path ended in a three-foot dive from a thin, rocky abutment to an ever-growing puddle on the chasm floor. He knelt, a smile spread wide across his face, and plunged both hands into the shallow crystalline pool. He splashed with joy and delight, letting the coolness soak his clothes without a trace of guilt or shame.

At last, the traveler lifted both hands to his mouth, careful not to overwhelm his quickly dehydrating body. Deeply he drank, slowly he swallowed, and immediately gagged. The water came up of its own accord; he coughed and wiped his face with trembling hands. *Slow down,* he implored himself and began again. The brown hands fell to the puddle once more, transformed themselves into a cup, and lifted the hidden treasure to his lips. He sipped, swirled the water around and about his mouth. There was a trace of unpleasantness there, a bite or a sting like foul, poison fire, and he spat the stuff upon the ground in disbelief.

His hand ignored the puddle, reaching for the slow downward trickle, and Arach let his fingers soak up the droplets from the chest-high waterfall. The hand bypassed his mouth this time, making a direct course for his nose. *Nothing*. He tasted and felt the obscene burn upon his tongue as before.

The traveler stepped from the puddle, placing both hands upon his hips. "What a cruel temptation," he muttered as his eyes scanned up and down the uneven surface of wall. His eyes fell to the canyon floor, to the lengthening shadows and the cloud-dotted blue sky above. He studied the curve of the wall, the sporadic shelves and porches of stone that hopped their ways here and there along the chasm wall. "Can I?" he whispered, not wanting to hear the unpleasant reaction of the pessimist within. "Should I?" he amended as he raised a wet, dripping hand to a sweaty brow in an attempt to scan the lower winding path through rocky crags ahead.

The hand dropped, the eyes lifted. He approached the wall, reaching out to it once more with both hands. He clung to it, dug his dirty calloused fingers deep within the cracks and crevices pitting its steep and solid face, placed his left foot on a crumbling shelf, and allowed his arms and leg to lift himself a foot above the ground. His right leg was next, and blindly, he searched for a foothold wide enough to suffice. Upward he climbed, one foot and one hand at a time, little by little, breath by dusty breath. With nowhere to rest, he continued to climb for the world above and beyond, to a land so far from reach and sight.

For hours he climbed, until the sky transformed into dangerous hues of reds and oranges, and the cracks in front of his face began to lose their shape and substance to the smear of ever-growing shadows. Even still, he climbed, for there was nothing more to do but climb, and in time, the welcoming chords of swift rushing water filled his ears from just beyond his sight. He clung to the glorious sound, reached out for it with his weary, fractured soul, until his left, then right hand grasped solid, flat ground. The traveler ignored the tense, jittery muscles telling his arms and legs to just give in, pulled himself up and over the ledge with a final painful heave, and fell face first in the welcome pillow of thick, green, beautiful grass.

*

The traveler awoke with the warmth of sun on his back, the sound of flowing water in his ears. Thirty minutes was all he needed, a welcome half hour to ignore the world, its troubles, and all his burgeoning cares. Arach lifted his head, filled his lungs with the scent of life, and opened hopeful eyes to the stream set before him.

It was close but not as near as he'd imagined - twenty yards or so distant from where he lay, a good twenty-five yards from cliff's edge just past his feet - and the first sight which caught his attention was the downed tree spanning one side of the stream to the other. "Not good," Arach groaned, knowing his first priority should be to solve the mystery of the gentle but poisonous trickle down the face of the steep chasm wall. Begrudgingly, he stood, stretched his arms and legs much as a feline would, and brushed himself off. His attention turned to the gaping wound in the earth and he breathed a grateful sigh of relief to be standing on open, elevated, grass-covered ground.

Arach searched the crumbling ledge for the rivulet in question, tracing its winding course through a miniature forest of grass, dirt, twigs, and stones. He took his time, ignoring the parched and burning throat that begged its host for just one sip of cool relief. "Not yet," he croaked hoarsely, his eyes at constant work to trace the thin, watery line along the ground. "Something isn't right. I just hope it's not-"

He stopped in his tracks, feeling the suction pull noisily at his boots in the stinking shallow mud he'd stepped into. His heart faltered and resumed its pace in double time. Face down in the muddy tributary was Rimmel, his empty, lifeless body sprawled grotesquely in the muck. "Oh, my friend," Arach whispered, ignoring the furious protest of his painful swollen throat. He knelt in the mud beside the tanner and felt the frigid wrist for a pulse that could not be found. "You did not deserve a fate such as this."

The presence split the stillness of the somber late afternoon, stretching the traveler's soul apart like the chasm at his rear. He had no need to look up from the bloated corpse to know whose stench it was that filled his flaring nostrils. "It was not your choice, Arach, but mine."

"And what did he do," the traveler lashed out in contempt, "that you should rob his life not once but twice?"

The wraith floated beyond arm's reach, staring at the shell of a man in the mud. "He did not please me."

He ignored the heartless words as he strained

against the debilitating mud and rolled the tanner onto his back. The torso was open to the world, its blackened contents spilled carelessly into the meandering tributary. Arach held back a retch, imagining the same filth filling his mouth and throat on the canyon floor. "Was he nothing more than a pawn in your cruel, vile game to ensnare me?" The being remained still, silent. Carefully, Arach grabbed both legs and pulled the cold lifeless body from the shallows.

"And what comes next?" the shadow asked from its place near canyon's edge. "Will you build another ramshackle cart to haul the rotting corruption halfway across the world?"

"I will bury him." He glared knives of acrimony into the immoral darkness and bowed his head, staring into the dead, milky eyes of a man he never knew existed a day before. "For even the dead deserve a trace of honor and respect at the end of it all."

The wraith moved closer, its icy breath cold upon the kneeling man. "And what would you dig his grave with, human?"

He gritted his teeth, disgusted and sick of the unwelcome visitor. "A stone. My fingers. Anything I can find. It matters not to me."

"You would do such a thing for a man who offered you up as a sacrifice? For a man who wanted you dead this same day?"

Arach stood to his feet, pulled the cloak from his ruined, weary frame, and wrapped the corpse as best he could. He removed the knife from his side and plunged it deep into the earth. Down the blade fell again and again until the soil had turned enough to allow the blade a rest. He dug his hands into the dirt, lifting the damp soil from the earth in clumps and clods one armful at a time.

"You have seen my work, human." The wraith hovered close, touching the earth with its extended tendril. "Shall I ease your burden?"

Furiously, he dug, palms and fingers full of dirt and pooling blood, until he paused long enough to spit vehemence at the foot of the hovering apparition. "You can ease my burden by tossing yourself into the water and ridding the earth of yourself."

He continued to dig in silence, ignoring the cold, hateful presence hovering just beyond his aching shoulder. In time, the evening warmth returned, the stench of evil washed fast and far away in its welcome wake. At last, under the shadow of setting sun, the traveler pulled the stiffening legs forward and into the shallow grave unfit for beast, much less tragic departed human.

Arach stood at the head of the hole a moment longer, wondering if the tanner had a wife, a home, or children of his own. He shook his head and pushed the dirt into the makeshift grave, the dirty laborious task his best and only gift to offer the fallen man named Rimmel. The traveler found the largest stone within sight and placed it gently upon the grass-less mound of earth and hidden death. "May we meet again in greener, peaceful lands, my friend."

Chapter Seventeen

Sy-i was correct: as the first sliver of impending dawn cracked the black eastern sky, a horn broke the stillness of a short, restless night. Heralds and runners ordered all men not actively on watch duty to abandon sleep and make for the open training ground.

"You should all know the drill by now," Captain Hemas shouted from a short, elevated platform, the tall eastern wall serving as his only backdrop. "Work within your squads, focus only on the tasks assigned to your particular team. Easy enough?" A uniform chant of *Aye!* resonated from the crowded, dusty square of sleep-deprived men. "Our rally point will be the glade beyond the western gate. I expect each of you to be there standing at attention one hour from now. You will await further orders at that time." He studied the crescendo of colors at his back, squinted at the rapidly rising sun, and returned both eyes to the field of men before him. "Time is precious, soldiers. You are dismissed."

Tiro was affixed to the earth, letting the rush of men flow to his left and right. Most officers waited for the men to disperse, their faces lifted to the platform and their heads nodding in time to their own specific orders doled out by the now kneeling captain. The hunter took a cautious step forward, catching the eye of the red-haired commander. Tiro saw Cephan's head lean in toward the captain. Unheard words were muttered between the two older men and the boy was beckoned to approach the stage. "Captain?" he asked self-consciously, unable to ignore the dozen or so pair of officerial eyes following his slow path forward. "A word if I may?"

Hemas studied a creased document, signed it with a flourish, and handed it to an unarmed boy not half of Tiro's age. The captain gave his full attention to the bowman. "Quite a busy night, wasn't it?"

Flustered, the boy lifted a hand and ran it across his sweat-beaded forehead. "Yes, sir. It's only..."

"Perhaps I can finish your thought: you assume I've forgotten all about you. Am I on the right track?"

"Well...sort of, yes."

The captain leapt from the two-foot-high platform and dismissed the lingering officers with a final order and a single clap. Cephan remained behind, leaned comfortably against the stage, and crossed his arms at the chest. "You couldn't be further from the truth. Do you see that runner over there?"

Tiro caught a glimpse of the young boy bearing the document the captain had just signed. "Yes, sir."

"He's gone to fetch your team."

Taken aback, Tiro opened his mouth in disbelief and shut it once again before finding a semi-stable voice. "M-my team, sir?"

Hemas smirked, patted the boy firmly on the shoulder, and nodded to Cephan, who filled in the details for the captain. "Technically, it's my team for now, so let's not get any funny ideas." The commander pushed himself from the platform and rested both thumbs inside his dark leather belt. "That includes any and all kinds of questionable tree activities, if you understand my meaning."

The boy nodded sharply, letting the captain proceed next. "There will be fifteen of you, not including the commander here. Ten bows and five swords for maximum speed. Commander Cephan will oversee you and the team for the time being, then turn command over to you as soon as you've proven yourself. Your objective will always be the same: to work with speed and operate in stealth. You're ghosts, Tiro, and your job - as a team, mind you - is to haunt the Empire."

"I can do that," he answered, the pride within swelling visibly.

"Wraith Squad is the title of this particular team," the captain said as he lifted a hand to beckon the first arrival. "And this is your first charge."

Tiro turned, recognizing the one-eyed bowman from the night before. "Sy-i," he greeted the man with a nod, who graciously returned the favor.

"I see you've found your place." The archer grinned and rubbed both hands together, clearly pleased to have been singled out.

"And I see someone is excited to have gotten out of tear-down duty," Cephan added before directing a handful of newcomers to join the ragtag collection of Wraiths. The two highest-ranking officers waited for all others to arrive and allowed each man to introduce himself, a task more for Tiro's sake than their own.

"So here's the plan: as soon as we're debriefed, the sixteen of us will leave camp and turn to the north." Cephan knelt in the dirt, drawing a crude map with his gloved right hand. "Our new camp is in this vicinity, about a full day's march northeast of here." He drew a line straight up from their current location, connecting it to an X denoting the new location of camp. "Our brothers in camp will take the easy route. We, on the other hand, get to go the fun way."

Captain Hemas stepped forward, removing a knife from his boot. With it, he drew three small triangles in the map, each point hugging the northern line drawn by Commander Cephan. "There are three imperial outposts right here, here, and here." He stabbed each triangle for added effect. "These need to go. Two of them are small, nothing more than under-manned checkpoints through the woods that lead to our third, most vital target." Hemas pointed to the northernmost triangle, the point where the straight line ended. "Anyone know what this is?"

Attention fixed upon the crudely sketched map of dirt, one of the swordsmen spoke up. "Could be the Suzu-Fiyimi Crossroads."

"Very good," the captain answered, well pleased with the clean-shaven soldier. "We need to take it from them, drive them further north, and push them out of the area entirely."

Tiro scratched his chin, pondering the distance

between the crossroads and the new camp location to its west.

"Once you secure this point - this crossroads - you wait." Captain Hemas looked up at last, fixing Tiro with a steady stare. "There is plenty of cover, plenty of trees. After your first strike, rid the roads of the dead and pick off any imperials who find themselves lucky enough to be passing through. There will be plenty to keep you occupied for a day or two at most."

Grunts sounded from the men around the circle, a chorus of clear understanding.

"Our brothers to the east will rendezvous with you at the crossroads as soon as time allows. My best estimate is one to two days." Hemas stood to his feet, trampling the map under foot. "Once they have arrived and secured the crossroads for *The Hand,* they will raise their own camp and set armed waypoints throughout the region. You will remain at your post until the following morning, then rejoin us in our new camp to await your next assignment. Any questions?"

Only a hundred or so, Tiro thought. He kept his mouth sealed shut, eyes fixed upon the captain's bearded chin.

"Then get to it, men." He looked each man in the eye, ending with the young hunter. "And remember: you are invisible, you are ghosts. You are wraiths who haunt the enemy."

Wraiths. Tiro nodded, the confidence returning where doubt had tried to corrupt. *Yes, I can do this.*

*

He washed his hands in a meandering forest stream, scrubbing the dry, blackened blood from beneath his fingernails. "I only wish we could leave them for the dogs."

"If only." Cephan stood with one foot upon a stone, massaging his elbow with his bare left hand. Behind the two men, sounds of steady digging and whispered conversation. The commander shook his head, attentively scanning the brook and forest beyond the preoccupied hunter. "But we mustn't leave any trace, so it's into the ground they go."

Tiro studied his arms and hands, scratched a lonely fleck of blood from his wrist, and switched places with the red-haired commander. His sight was drawn well past the swaying forest heights, straight to the rapidly descending sun high up its heavenly perch. "Ten graves take too much time to dig. I was hoping to reach the second checkpoint before sundown."

Cephan dipped both arms in the frigid water, uncontrollably wincing from the shock. The blood flowed off his body in two thick rivulets, vanishing deep within the gentle downstream flow. "What do you think? Should we split the men up, sending half on their way north?"

The hunter returned his eyes to the waterlogged officer, wondering if the question was a trap or test of some sort. "No. We should stick together. I'll help the men dig as soon as you're done."

The commander cracked a ghost of a smile, nodding. "Sounds good to me."

The dirty, bloody burial process took longer than expected. At last, the final scoop of dirt fell, the sixteen rebels covered head to toe in mud, muck, and crusted sweat. Tiro found the sun, estimating the men had an hour and a half of sunlight left at most. "Let's follow the stream for a mile or two, clean up, and make camp for the night." He looked upon the ten haunting mounds of dirt set thirty feet in from the winding forest road. A shiver ran down his aching spine, and he turned his eyes from the cursed burial ground. "I have no desire to sleep amongst the dead tonight."

Morning came, and with it, another slow and steady trek through the sleepy ancient forest. Silently, they prowled, sixteen shadows spread two hundred yards apart, and made no sound save the constant drumming of anxiously pounding hearts. No disruption greeted them that morning save the occasional flap of wings overhead and the panicked scurry of frightened climbing squirrels. Their voices were their hands, fingers, and wide eyes. Each kept in constant contact with the fellow to his right and left.

Eventually, a foreign, unwelcome sound shattered the stillness, a grating noise reserved for those too arrogant and unconcerned to care. Tiro glanced left then right, received nods from both comrades, and watched the mutual wave of concurrence continue as far down the line as the eye could see. Further to his right, Cephan lifted a clenched fist, extended his forefinger and pinky, then traced an invisible circle in the air with his raised index finger. The order was efficiently passed down the line and each man clearly understood the command: the furthest wings of the line would move forward as the center held back, enabling the silent squad of rebels to encircle the enemy checkpoint and surround it from all sides.

After an hour of impatiently waiting on the forest floor with his back to a tree, Tiro heard the musical trill of an imaginary forest bird fill his ears. He responded in kind and heard the pleasant sound echo far to his right. The hunter pushed himself from the earth, sheathed his bow across his back, and faced the mammoth tree that kept him company for the last torturous hour. Up its trunk he climbed, cautiously, noiselessly, until his view was perfectly unobstructed and he was able to wrap both legs around a large, horizontal limb with his back to the tapering trunk. From the heights he saw them; bored, uncaring soldiers bearing accursed triple markings of the Empire. The hunter strained, searched, and counted each one, recounted, and found a fool worthy enough to bear the first mark of death. It would be the bloody signal his fellow brothers sought to commence their own devastating attack.

He wiped the sweat from his brow. There were not many, eleven or twelve, he guessed, but there were two pockets of brush and a stationary wagon - empty, he could tell - that could very well be hiding another two to three imperials from sight. *No more time,* his internal clock warned and he awakened the bow from its resting place. The bowstring brushed his cheek and he struggled against its pull. Breath held fast, he aimed and fired. The arrow pinged sharply against the crimson-stained chest plate and the blood splattered the ground mere moments before the body fell. Tiro hoped the ping was loud enough for the men to hear, drew another arrow, and steadied himself from a near fall from the heights.

The whoosh of arrows split the air; he added another to the fracas. More blood, more muted cries of pain, and in an instant, the clearing was littered with the dead and dying. Still, three remained unharmed and each tossed his weapon to the ground in a clear sign of abject surrender. Surrounded and outnumbered, each man knew there was simply no escape.

Pulse pounding, Tiro lowered his bow with a curse and studied the work of art strewn clear across the forest floor. *Three more!* he shouted inwardly, wishing he had drawn fast enough to get one or two more deadly shots off.

"Well, that was easy." From behind the wagon, Cephan approached the crouching prisoners, sheathed his bloody sword, and kicked the three abandoned weapons far beyond the reach of huddled soldiers. "What can I say? Today is not your lucky day, boys." He waited for the three imperial soldiers to raise subservient heads and gazed into their frightened eyes as light streamed down from silent forest eaves. "Today, you were bested by ghosts. We are wraiths who take no captors."

With a smirk, Tiro drew the string toward himself, propelling the missile forward with a joyous yelp. He lowered the bow, watching as three more imperial scum breathed their final breaths at the feet of the red-haired commander.

Chapter Eighteen

"You're afraid."

Arach smoothed the beard that framed his face and let his heavy-lidded eyes fall to the mud-encrusted boots and trousers that he wore. Without the need to observe himself in the nearby stream's reflection, he knew he resembled a road worn vagrant, a wandering nomad. "Do you ever close your mouth?" he called over his shoulder as his attention returned to the town in the distance. "Do you ever tire of planting seeds of fear and digging holes in unwelcome gardens?"

Soft laughter filled the air, and the being glided forward. "I simply wish to fill your ears with truth."

"Your version of truth is nothing more than condemnation and judgment."

"Perhaps. But truth, at times, is a painful field

to sow and reap."

Weary eyes shifted from the north-facing towers and elevated platforms to the traffic flowing in and out of the wide, open gate. Man and beast alike wandered here and there near the crowded entrance of town like dark, winding trails of hard-working ants; countless travelers, merchants, beggars, and traders scurried in and out, each one going about their own personal business like the busy worker ants they were.

Beyond the wooden wall were pointed peaks of houses piercing the sky, narrow empty spaces where roads and alleys crisscrossed around the multi-storied buildings. He could feel the thinness of air down there, could sense the compact, crowded space forbidding room to move and freely live. It had been so long since he'd visited a town of any size, and a smothering sense of claustrophobia had just then taken root. "Everything about you is painful, wraith," he said and nodded his head in the direction of the walled-in town. "Do you ever visit places like these? Roam the streets at night and torment children as they try their best to sleep?"

"On occasion," it hissed, the glee apparent in the sickening words it spoke. The wraith said no more.

Arach looked past the town to the sea at its

southern foot. It sparkled in the late afternoon light and he breathed a sigh of relief for a journey on the brink of near completion. Home was close, within his grasp. War-torn and damaged that land beyond his sight might surely be, but home was home, a place of warmth and comfort and rest. "One more night, wraith," he spoke aloud, more to himself than the nearby apparition at his side. "You've been hounding my trail for much too long. Perhaps now would be as good a time as any to say farewell?"

With a breeze upon his back, Arach turned to face the lightless being on his left. The rustle of nearby treetops, the steady rush of water, and the distant neigh of an impatient horse gave the only answers. He turned around, from left to right, and faced the gloomy wooden town. Once again, he was all alone.

*

"Name?"

"Arach, son of Anak. From Fiyimi across the sea."

The middle-aged, grey-haired guard at the gate looked him up and down, furrowing his brow. "What's your business?"

He fought the urge to scratch his head and locked both hands behind his back. "On my way home from an errand up north."

The helmeted official had no trouble looking skeptical. "On foot?"

Arach nodded once, shifted his weight, and fixed his eyes on the back of another nearby inquisitor. "I, well...I misplaced my horse...and cart...three days ago."

"'Misplaced,' eh?" The guard waited for the traveler to nod. "You know gambling is illegal in this town, Arach, son of Anak?" Another nod. "So don't go trying to replace your *missing* horse with an illegal game of dice, will you? No second warnings, traveler. Our jail is overflowing with plenty of foreigners just like you. Understood?"

He nodded and took a tentative step through the open gate. "And the nearest inn?" The guard pointed straight down the main thoroughfare, shifting his needlepoint focus on the next visitor in queue. "Thank you, sir," Arach added, a parting farewell immediately lost in the shuffle of men and madness.

And just like that he was tossed into the stream of men and stone, a fragile leaf floating south through a wash of travelers much akin him. From memory, he was reminded of the gloves he had lost to the swiftly moving stream just days before, wondering where their watery path had taken them. Would anyone find them, wonder who had left the frayed accessories behind? Would they be lost forever, swallowed by earth and grass, or taken all the way to sea to drown within?

The dangling wood and metal sign came into sudden view and Arach angled himself awkwardly through the mass of men, women, children, beasts, and carts. He pulled his shoulders in and muttered apology after unanswered apology for the bumps and stumbles caused in the overly crowded street. At last, he threw himself through the open doorway of an inn hugging the corner of the cold cobblestone street, breathed a sigh of relief, and adjusted his dirty, dusty clothes with a shake of the head.

"Busy this time of day," a man behind a dimly lit counter laughed as he poured drink after drink and set each dripping mug of ale onto a faded red tray. "What can I do for you?"

Arach looked around the tavern and let his eyes adjust to the dimness of a low, windowless room. Rickety tables littered the floor and the feeble light pouring through the doorway revealed a floor sticky and discolored from countless drinks spilled throughout the ages. The smell of roasting meat beyond an open kitchen door filled his nose and his stomach answered wildly. The table to his immediate right was too great a temptation and he took a much-needed seat. "A meal and a drink first, if you don't mind. Then a room for the night if one is still available."

"So long as you have the coin." The man smiled before turning his attention to the far side of the room. In an instant, his cheerful demeanor was tossed out the window like a bucket of waste. "Still alive over there? What's keeping you?"

Laughter and chatter from the furthest table shattered the peace as a figure was pushed and stumbled from the seated cluster of men. "Hurry back!" one called and the others added similar catcalls of their own.

He watched her cross the room, saw her trembling hand lift to straighten stray strands of long black hair behind an ear the same dark shade of brown as his own. Her eyes, too, that same familiar shape and color always greeting him at stream's edge. The traveler fought the urge to rise, step forward, and ask her name.

"Take care of our new guest," the man behind the counter ordered the girl before gesturing to the tray full of mugs, "and get these to our friends in the corner. Hurry now."

She straightened her shoulders, taking an almost imperceptible breath. The girl turned from the counter with eyes downcast, approaching the table with a thin, pasted-on smile. "Welcome, traveler. How can I help you?"

Tongue-tied, he studied the shadowed youthful face. Sadness was there, a world of loneliness and despair. Her delicate neck was bruised yellow and purple on both sides, the tip of a gash along her collarbone showing just above the hem of dual violet and dark purple robes. He opened his mouth, the words escaping him. Her eyes lifted from his chest to his chin, and she gave a start and a frown, and two pair of dark, confused eyes met for the first time. Arach noticed the quiver of her lip and saw the eyes begin to mist over as they dropped to the more comfortable spot on his chest.

A pound from across the room startled both from wordless stupor. "Aren't those drinks ready yet, girl?" a voice from the raucous table asked.

She drew another smile upon her face, the joy of which failed to reach her eyes. "Forgive me, friends; I'll be there soon enough!"

Arach glanced past the girl to the man behind the counter and deflected his deadly impatient glare with a look of his own. The girl's attention returned to him. "What smells so good in the back?"

"Ah...stew, sir. Can I get you some?"

"Please." He nodded, stammering about for something more to say. "Can I ask a question?" The distraught eyes lifted again, a wordless plea for silence. He ignored the request and continued on. "What brings you across the sea?"

Her mouth opened and the hand returned to the long, luxurious hair. A cackle from behind the counter shattered his focus and Arach looked up to see the innkeeper smirking. "She just arrived two days ago. Never had another like her on this side of town, so I crossed the sea and bought her at auction. Thought she'd be a bit rare and exotic...but now there's two of you in the same room and I feel like I may have been bamboozled!" The man reached for a mug, polished it off with a grimy towel, and grinned. "Not such a big deal, I suppose, so long as you have no plans on sticking around for long. Supply and demand, you know?"

Speechless, Arach looked from the man to the girl, back again once more.

"Got her for a pittance, if you want to know the truth. Still...what are the chances of two of you in the same inn, what with the war going on and all?"

The girl stood stock still, the men in the corner more agitated by the minute. Arach looked from the drunks to the girl to the man, swallowed the lump of anger and humiliation in his throat, and made his decision. "So how much for a room and the girl to go with it?"

She turned a deep shade of crimson as the man's grin widened above a pair of busy hands stacking bowls and plates with meticulous care. "Depends on how long we're talking, my friend."

He touched the much neglected pouch at his hip, considered what remained, and said an easy farewell to the hard-earned coin. "All night."

"Missing home that much, eh?" the man asked.

The traveler leaned back in his chair, considered the cruelty of life and the men who made it worse. He felt the girl's fear, envisioning the final agonizing breath his wife had sighed in a life cut much too short by men such as these. "I'll be taking my meal upstairs as well."

"You heard him, girl," the man said, his voice uprooting her from the spot she'd claimed tableside.

Arach stood, approached the counter, and placed a stack of coins one atop the other before the innkeeper. The traveler turned his back to the room and heard a drunkard shout, "And what about our tray of drinks, man?"

The soft clink of coins chased him halfway up the stairs, the last words of the slave owner not too far behind. "You have legs. Come and get them yourselves."

*

The doorknob turned with a frightening

squeak, the door opening inward to the small room. A lighted candle perched upon a smooth blue desk beside the doorway flickered from the sudden movement and the drab room bowed before her vibrant shades of violet and purple. "Your food, sir," she said.

"Arach." The door closed behind her, and she bowed her head politely. "My name is Arach."

"You're hungry, Arach. You should eat."

He pushed himself from his spot against the wall and stood to his feet. He crossed the short distance to the girl, pulled a stool from underneath the desk, and motioned for her to take a seat. "I'm not going to hurt you. You can sit, eat. The food is for you."

"I...I can't, sir- I mean, Arach. This is yours. You have already paid for it."

The traveler removed the steaming bowl of stew from her hands and set it down upon the desk. "I'm afraid I've lost my appetite." He patted the stool with his hand, waving her forward. "Please, sit down." He crossed the room to the small space between the bed and the wall, resting his back against the peeling red planks.

The girl sat, facing the bowl with an arched back and eyes cast down. "Thank you, but I have no appetite either."

"Fair enough." He pulled his knees toward his

chest, wrapping both arms around them. "But may I ask your name?"

Her hand touched the spoon beside the bowl, toying with it for a moment in wordless thought. For the first time, he saw the cruel tattoo etched across her bare left wrist: three parallel strokes, the mark of a slave of the Empire. "I have no name anymore. Just *Girl*."

Arach stared at the markings and lifted his eyes to her slumped profile. "They took my wife from me as well." Her head moved, turning slightly toward him. "Not as a slave, but..."

The flame stirred, its dance the only movement in the suffocating room. The girl let her body shift in place on the stool, turning herself toward him. "I was with my mother when they killed her." Neither looked at the other, but at a dirty, frayed rug spanning the distance between them. "We were outside working the field; laughing, talking about dinner. Talking about my brother and another boy from our village. And then they came from nowhere." Her hand reached for the spoon and carried it to her lap. "There was nothing I could do. I could only stand there and watch."

Grief was their bond; a sacred, special thing. Arach let the silence hang, speaking his tale into existence. "I was away when it happened. The guilt was so strong, so overpowering. In truth, it still is.

It's what led me here across the sea." He awoke from the grievous trance and saw her eyes upon him. "So I know how your guilt consumes you-" He trailed off, unsure what to call her.

"Tara," she answered, her eyes lifting from the arms across his knees to his face.

"I know how your guilt consumes you, Tara. I struggle with it myself. The *what ifs* and the demons that haunt our thoughts both night and day." His gaze crossed the room to a chink in the shuttered window, a hopeful ray of light piercing through the semi-darkness. "But as difficult as it may seem, we must remind ourselves that their deaths were no fault of our own."

"And then what?" Tara leaned forward, an earnest grasp for the visiting ray of hope, and placed her slender arm along the surface of the desk. "How should a slave move on in life?"

The light faded, a cruel victim of a heartless passing cloud, and the candle cast its long, dreadful shadow across the girl's face. He slowly shook his head and let his vision fall to the rug beneath their feet. Both knew the question had no simple answer.

Chapter Nineteen

"We must tread carefully from here on."

Tiro leaned into the whispered words, scanning the stalwart faces of his fifteen comrades for any trace of fear or nerves. Each man - himself included - bore the restless emotions of fear and nerves, both as clear as a bright, cloudless day.

Beads of sweat dripped from Cephan's head, soaking into the dirt beside his bended knee. "My fear is the forest will be much too thick for stealth between here and there." He leaned forward, right arm at rest upon his elevated right knee, and peered through the dense foliage to the wide dirt road no further than a stone's throw away. "Therefore, I feel we should approach via the highway."

Each hot, humid breath was a constant struggle for the young hunter, yet the boy felt himself shiver with the cold, incredulous words. Beyond conscious thought, his eyes shifted to the half-blind archer Sy-i. Both men exchanged puzzled looks before returning their confused attention back upon the impassive leader. "In the open?" Tiro asked the westerner before a humorless bark of a laugh escaped his dry, cracked lips. "Can you tell us how that is supposed to work?"

"I know it seems odd, but hear me out. They aren't expecting us. From a distance, they'll assume we're travelers." He locked eyes with the brazen commander-in-training, the look he wore one of unquestionable confidence in his decision. "In boldness, we shall stay hidden."

Tiro shook his head, pounding the earth with gloved fist. "We have more than enough time to plan, Cephan-"

"I am your *commander*, Tiro, and you will address me as such."

He brushed the comment aside, pressing forward. "Forgive me. We have time, Commander. Time to organize an attack, time to get situated." He motioned to the sky full of branches overhead. "Time to get up there in the trees. Our best bet is to take them out from above and tempt those who remain into the woods so our swords can finish them off."

"If we do that, we'll have to tromp noisily through the woods first." Cephan pointed, the timbre of his voice rising slightly into realms of frustration and perturbance. "Straight and swift is the key here."

The young hunter shifted from an uncomfortable crouch to a kneeling position on bended knees. With his finger, he drew the intersection of roads in the near distance. "So let me get this straight. We are here. We leave the forest for the road, turn north," he drew a swift line up toward the crossroads, "and take out a few here." He stabbed at the three remaining roads facing west, north, and east. "Even if we take them by surprise and catch them off guard, all who remain will have three directions to flee. Or better yet, if they're smart, they'll simply draw us into the intersection and trap us all like a pack of rats."

"You overestimate your foe, Tiro," the commander answered before standing to his feet and refusing to meet the hunter's eye. "They are lazy, disorganized, and no match for us. Trust me; I've been fighting this foe for years now." He looked to his comrades for a mutual show of support. Each back hunched forward above the hastily drawn map, the weight of the dangerous task ahead bearing down mightily upon them.

Tiro pushed himself from the dirt, dusted

himself off, and allowed the others to rise before speaking again. "Very well, Commander, it's your call. If we're all ready," he continued, forbidding the gnawing sense of dread to take further root, "I say we get to it."

One by one, they exited the forest and onto the orange-brown highway bearing due north. Tiro stepped from the homely world of branch and leaf, placed a cautious foot upon the cold crushed stone, and fought back a wave of nausea as he glanced from north to south. The way was deserted, abandoned. Peaceful.

"Spread out," the order came from behind and Tiro watched as his nervous comrades took the words to heart. "No turning back now, men. Checkpoint stations on the left and right are straight ahead. Decide now: who wants left, who wants right?"

He listened to the assignments, flexed his tense shoulders, and cracked his knuckles.

"There are three more waystations just like the ones ahead. After we take care of the first pair, half of you will break to the west, the other half to the east. Kill the men on guard and any stragglers you may find. We'll form up in the middle and move on to the northern checkpoint. Understood?" All answered *Yes*. "There may well be another wave of imperials to stream out from the west. I believe that's where the barracks and stables are located."

Believe? Tiro repeated to himself, fighting against the burgeoning desire to hijack command and call the premature attack off at once. It was lunacy, suicidal.

And then the horrid sound he knew so well, the onrush of unnatural whistling wind, the dread that followed close behind. The first arrow hit, a white-hot sting of pain that penetrated deep into his left thigh, scraped against the bone, and poked its head out the back through muscle and skin. "Off the road!" Tiro screamed, the warning nothing more than a pitiful waste of breath and strength as he saw the enemy materialize from the woods and road ahead. He stumbled, screamed in torment as the shaft shifted painfully from the hard fall. Tiro stretched out his leg, twisted onto his right hip, and struggled in vain for the bow still sheathed at his back. The *whirring* sound came once again, he fell to the earth at the sight of a deadly volley of iron-tipped arrows.

A *whoosh* passed overhead, a thud to his left, and the clatter of wooden shafts skimming across stone further behind. "Hands up!" came the command from ahead. Tiro did as he was told, chanced a look to left and right on the northbound road. Three of his comrades sprawled unnaturally across the path, their bodies broken boats anchored deep in lakes of blood. The others stood with hands raised, two comrades sporting ugly flesh wounds such as his in arms and shoulder.

"You move, you die, rebels. Go ahead and test me." The voice came from a bareheaded soldier on horseback. Tiro watched as the bearded man issued indecipherable commands and waved four dozen or so archers, swordsmen, and axe-bearers to surround the helplessly trapped rebels. Movement from Tiro's right caught his eye, and he turned to face his commander. *I'm sorry*, the man mouthed, shook his head, and dropped a sorrowful face in defeat.

"You amateurs are getting predictable," the mounted officer scoffed with his approach. He pulled the steed to a halt and leapt from the chestnut mare. "Who's in charge here?"

Cephan lifted his head, meeting the stare of the brown-skinned man who bore the rank of captain on his shoulder. "That would be me."

The imperial officer approached with wonder in his face and sped up his confident, arrogant gait. "And a westerner at that! Look at him, men," he addressed his fellow soldiers who crowded the highway in a circle around the rebels. "I don't believe Major Raik has a trophy quite like this one." He stepped forward, reaching his left hand out for the wavy locks of red hair falling in a sweat-drenched waterfall around the rebel commander's face. With his right, he withdrew the sword at his side and plunged the blade hilt-deep into Cephan's stomach. "Arrogant pig," he spat and twisted the blade a quarter turn before pulling it out of the blooming circle of red with a swift kick of his heel. The captain allowed Cephan to collapse upon the stone-covered road, watched him writhe in voiceless pain, and hacked down at the unprotected neck. In unmasked shock and horror, Tiro watched the imperial officer reach down with a laugh, pick up the head, and toss it to a nearby soldier. "Find a jar and send it north to the Major."

Tiro fell back to reality. Warm blood seeped into his trousers, a steady drip from the burning wound in his thigh. Lightheaded, he began to waver where he sat, feeling his arms pull as weights toward the spinning earth.

"How does it feel to be betrayed?" the captain asked rhetorically as he strode up the line of rebels, the sword in hand as crimson as the triple markings of the Empire upon his chest. "To have your very lives stripped from you by the ineptness of a man you once called leader? Well?" He paused before a rebel swordsman, lopping the man's head off with a single stroke. The body toppled, both men beside it showered in a horrid gush of blood and gore. "You think you can stand against the might of an Empire fueled and funded by royalty?"

Silence greeted each question, no sound to be heard at all save the soft crunch of gravel and heavy labored breathing of the hopelessly surrounded rebels. Weary, Tiro lifted his head and saw the captain had reached the end of the line of captors. The man stopped, leaned in to the stock-still head of Sy-i and peered into the face of a statue. "Are times so bad for you rebels that *The Hand* now hires one-eyed archers? Or did they simply assume the mythical Cyclops had at last been found closer to home than ever expected?" The men around him laughed, as did he. "So tell me, Cyclops: was yours a wound suffered in battle against the Empire? Against the rightful emissaries of the king himself?"

Sy-i lifted his head and spat in the face of the captain. The officer held his left hand to the sky, a direct order to halt a violent retaliation from a nearby soldier. He sheathed his bloody sword and ripped the quiver of arrows from the archer's side. With a vicious yank, he withdrew one and tossed the leather bag to the road. "Look at me, traitor," the imperial captain commanded the one-eyed rebel as he grabbed Sy-i's chin in a vise-like grip, "and remember my face. It is the last thing you will ever see in this life." He lifted the arrow, plunged it into the seeing eye of the archer, and withdrew it with a firm tug. "Bandage him up and strip him of his cloak and chain mail. Leave the traitor alive to wander in darkness for the rest of his poor, unfortunate days on earth."

Tiro pried his eyes from the cursed, bloody arrow, willing a flood of tears to stay within his glassy, hate-filled eyes.

Above the blind archer's wail, the captain continued: "Kill the remaining swordsmen and every other archer. Remove the first two joints of each finger from the ones you keep alive." He turned to face his horse, calling out a final order to his men: "And get the bodies off the road. We wouldn't want to frighten away any innocent travelers, would we?"

A final frantic rustling was followed by a violent slaughter. All was deathly silent. Still alive, Tiro lowered his hands, wiped a swath of blood from his face and studied the trembling fingers he'd always taken for granted. A pair of legs filled Tiro's vision, a sword unsheathed and placed beneath his chin. "On your knees and hands flat on the ground, rebel," the imperial soldier ordered as he lifted the boy's head.

"Wait!" a voice cried from Tiro's right, a note of astonishment in the sudden exclamation. "Captain, a moment if you will, sir?"

The sword nicked the hunter's throat, a sharp

sting that preceded a warm trail of blood chasing gravity beneath the folds of his dark green cloak.

"Speak up, soldier. I have more pressing matters to attend to. What is it?"

"The archer there," the voice beyond his line of sight announced in somewhat timid fashion. "The one with the arrow in his thigh."

"What about him?" the captain asked as he mounted the waiting horse, adjusting the cloak at his back.

"It's him, sir. *The Ghost*. The bowman with the bounty on his head. I'm sure of it, Captain."

Tiro felt the scrutiny upon him, heard a dull kick, and the sound of beast and man approach. The front legs of the horse came into view, stopped, and the beast's whinny touched his quivering cheek like a warm, unwanted caress. He lifted heavy-lidded eyes to the captain, swaying through a vicious bout of lightheadedness.

"My man says you're the one they call *The Ghost*," the officer asked with a smirk, both hands still adjusting himself in the jewel-encrusted saddle. "Well? What do you say about that? Is it true?"

He stared in silence, defiance his sacred weapon of choice.

"Do you not value your own life, boy?" He leaned forward, the outright belligerence and doubtful glare a mockery to the hunter. "I want an answer! Or would you prefer to bleed your worthless life into the dirt as you choke upon your own severed fingers?" He drew the sword from his side and kicked the horse forward. "Tell me now: are you *The Ghost?*"

Tiro closed his eyes, lifting his head to the beating sun upon his face. He welcomed it, craved it, let it warm him in the final moments of a restless, unfinished life. He sensed a familiar presence, felt his childlike hands wrapped tightly around those cold iron nails, heard the sound of a flat-headed hammer pound loudly within his father's strong hand. He smiled, the peace he sought in life a hair's breadth away. "Call me what you will, dog. I am Tiro, son of Torin; enemy of the Empire, warrior of *The Hand* as my father was before me; forsworn to-"

The flat of the blade appeared from nowhere, knocking the bowman to the earth with a splatter of spit and blood. Eyes open, his vision spun and flickered about in a kaleidoscope of painful colors. With what little strength remained, Tiro lifted himself to upright knees, gritting through the pain in head, leg, and aching heart.

"Soldier!" the captain called over his shoulder as he re-sheathed the vibrating sword. "Look him in the eye and tell me for certain: is this boy *The*

Ghost?"

Tiro followed the scuffling feet along the road, lifting painful eyes to the cruel symbol of imperial injustice. Further upward, his sight wandered to the wide, frightened eyes in the center of a helmetless head - eyes that refused to meet his own. *No!* he screamed, unsure if the word was spoken aloud or not, and the earth beneath him shifted, tumbled, and forced him back upon his face. He struggled for breath, inhaled the dust and grime at his lips, and let the darkness sink its welcome claws into his hopeless, battered soul.

A well-worn boot nudged him onto his back, the face of the captain blocking the beautiful rays of sun. His vision filled with nothing more than the terrible scowl of a blood-covered madman. "Well, Marik? Is it him?"

There was no hesitation. "It is, sir."

"Then dress his wound," the captain answered and ordered the removal of fingers to commence for the remaining bowmen. "But don't touch this one just yet. He's going north."

The betrayal echoed in his head and pierced his broken heart. Marik turned his back, dragging Cephan's headless body from the bloodstained road to the overgrowth of brush and vine on forest's edge.

Tiro closed his eyes to daylight, the world

vanished like a ghost.

Chapter Twenty

A pounding on the door woke him from an oddly peaceful sleep. Arach sat up from his place beside the bed, looking into a pair of frightened eyes as Tara pulled the tattered blanket up and to her nose. "Who is it? What do you want?" he spoke loud enough for his voice to carry through the latched door.

"Half an hour left, sir," the innkeeper announced with mischief in his voice, "unless you'd like to slide a coin beneath the door to pay for a bit more time."

The blanket fell to her chin, the ruffled surface of the bed a vision of rolling waves on a storm-tossed ocean. The girl stretched beneath its folds, a castaway adrift. She propped herself up on elbows, stifling a yawn behind lifted hand. Arach glimpsed the tattoo and rubbed the sleep from his own face.

"Thank you," he stated to the imploring innkeeper, no other words necessary just then.

The girl threw the blanket from the bed and moved to its edge, where she remained inert and motionless. Arach's eyes drifted to the empty bowl of stew, thought back to the recent hours shrouded now in memory. They had spoken of their pasts, their families, their faraway villages. Although the two had never met in life, they shared memories of people, places, and events nearer to home. The night was a comfort, the conversation a stimulus that brought their appetite for food back in a welcome flood. The pair shared the bowl of stew and soon fell asleep - Arach on the floor, Tara on the bed.

"Will you go home?" she asked, her body rigid as she sat unmoving on the bed.

The candle had long since died; he looked at the hardened puddle of wax and the small flameless nub in its center. The night was much too short, its passage a frail pane of quickly cracking glass. Arach nodded, placed both hands on the floor, and pushed himself up the wall. "I must."

Tara turned her head, studying the intricate designs of the twisted blanket beneath her. "My brother..."

"Tiro?"

She nodded, a flicker of joy bursting from her

eyes at the sound of his name and the fact that the traveler had listened intently and remembered so well. "He may still be alive, but...I don't know for certain."

"I will try to find him." He crossed the room, dipped his hands in a bowl of water on a counter, and washed his neck, beard, and face. His hands found a towel draped nearby, and he dried himself off. He did not want to face her, nor look upon her back. Still, Arach turned and observed the jet-black waterfall of loosely braided hair, its path a smooth, swift descent from forlorn crown to tangled bedsheets. "What should I tell him?"

She considered the question in reticence, stood to her feet, and arranged the bed. "Tell him...tell him that I am happy." She smiled a melancholy smile, her mind in a distant land across the sea. "And safe."

Arach crossed the room and knelt to retrieve his belt and small items from the floor. They were all he had left from the long journey. His hand reached for the tanner's knife, fingering its razor-sharp blade and simple hilt. He grabbed it by the blade, holding it out to her. "Is there a place you can hide this? Someplace safe and out of sight, of course."

The girl stared at the faded leather hilt, stepping forward with arms crossed beneath her chest. "I have a room. It's small, but…" She looked at the crack under the door, saw no shadow of feet, no lingering presence. "But it's my own. I found a loose plank in the floor."

He held his breath, stretched it further toward her, and exhaled as her arms uncrossed and reached for the proffered blade. Arach returned to what remained of the pile, unfurled the belt, and handed it to her as well. "Perhaps you can use this to hide it beneath your robes...for now, at least."

"Your kindness-" she began and bowed her head, unable to continue. The tattooed wrist lifted to her eyes and dried a stream of tears cascading down her cheeks. "I will not forget you, Arach."

The traveler tucked what few belongings remained into his pockets, crossed the room, and paused with hand on the cold, bulbous doorknob. "And neither shall I forget you." Pure morning light filled the room, the girl's mournful face half-illuminated. He closed the door behind him softly, her sorrow an image seared painfully across his soul.

*

Arach walked through lonely, deserted streets, neglected piles of trash and filth ignored as he stepped across each one. Troubled mind still fixed upon the girl, he kept both eyes on drab cobblestones worn smooth from relentless tread of feet and slow strain of time. Like flattened stones underfoot, he felt his soul was trampled, beaten, and abused. He longed for days when life was hope and love was young, when the same soul within his chest was shiny, smooth, and polished. When had the deterioration begun? Try as he might, the elusive transformative moment escaped him.

He turned a narrow corner and saw the wide southern gate not too distant, the choppy sea beyond. Ferries queued and fishermen's sails rustled further out in the distance. A seaside bell tolled its final warning for boarders of an unknown ship, its final destination uncertain. His eyes lifted to the heavens, finding the sun in its peaceful realm of blue. *Plenty of time to spare,* he knew.

Not far from the gate, a colorful sign drew his attention. Edged in green with a center of fading yellow, two horses - one brown, one black - stood majestic on hind legs with front hooves in the air. With an hour or more to spare until his ferry pushed off from shore, he made for the door and crossed the stable's threshold into a wide low-roofed barn, its creaking wooden floor covered in hay.

"Hello there, sir," rang a young man's voice

from an empty stall. The stable hand ceased his chore and leaned upon an unseen broom. "You're up early. What can I do for you?"

"Killing time for the most part." Arach walked up the wide central aisle, the stalls to left and right full of horses and mules separated by low stomach-high walls. "But I'd be interested in your prices if-" He stopped dead in his tracks, mouth falling agape in implausible surprise. "Yuzy!" He was at the stall in an instant, his faithful companion's head bobbing up and down in joy equal to its master. Arach turned to the man still leaning against the broom and laughed. "Incredible! Where did you find him? I lost him days ago in an accident!"

Sour grimace on his face, the young man answered, "Fella brought him in a couple of days ago. Says he found him running wild north of here. So long as you have the coins, he's yours." He resumed his chore in the stall ahead, the words a direct challenge to pay up or move along.

Arach reached into his pocket, pulled out what coins remained and counted them. He set aside what was needed for the long ferry ride home. "How much?"

"A hundred silver. If he really *was* yours, you know that's a steal of a price."

He clasped his hand around the coins, staring deep into the beast's elated eyes. "I have sixty.

Can't we deal?"

"I paid seventy for the animal, sir. Can't lose money - you know that." The man's eyes had yet to lift from the floor of the stall he furiously swept.

Hope escaped him with a groan. "Would you believe I spent an unforeseen fortune last night?"

"So long as it was on a girl," the stable hand answered, "I suppose you ain't got a right to complain."

His hands brushed the neck and hair, fingers scratched lovingly behind both ears. The beast stomped, ready to leave that instant, anxious to return to the grass and fields beyond. "I'm sorry, old boy. Looks like this is farewell," he whispered into an excited twitching ear. Arach looked around the stable, saw baskets of apples piled high beside an empty counter. "How much for one of those?" he pointed with his head.

"Fifty bronze for ten."

He reached into his pocket, crossed the aisle and removed the coins, set them on the counter as the man observed. The traveler returned to the stall, set the basket down at his feet, and fed the beast the first fruit from his hand. "I'm leaving too much behind on this old island, Yuzy." His companion devoured the apple, nudging him gently for another. He acquiesced, lifted it to the mouth. "Take care of yourself, old boy. I'm sure you'll find a good master. Treat him just as you did me, you hear?" He lifted the basket into the stall, setting it down at the feet of the beast. "And watch out for *you-know-who*. He's still lurking about somewhere. If you see him, give him a bite for me, will you?" A final pat on the neck and he thanked the stable owner, forcing himself to ignore the sounds of nervous protest from the stall behind.

The cool morning air and airborne cries of seagulls greeted his exit from the stable. A somber sigh escaped his lips and Arach massaged his grieving heart. He wanted to run, to slice and flee the shroud of depression about the town, to spit the foul taste of despair from his mouth. He hated the place, how it made him feel. Instead, he walked, setting his sights upon the sea.

He passed beneath the gate unmolested, following the rocky path to shore. To his right, the stream. Arach watched it empty itself into the massive body of water, its journey a long and arduous one from snow-peaked mountains to sun-kissed seashore. How it had kept and sustained him for mile after mile, its purity a giver of life, assurance, direction.

The long wooden pier to his left, the stream still at his right, he sat at water's edge and gazed into the distance. Home was somewhere beyond; unseen, yet he could still feel its gentle, loving tug.

"Stay."

He flinched and exhaled through clenched teeth. "Why would I?"

The morning light was swallowed within, its blackened cavity a slow, tar-like swirl. "There is still much to do."

"Sometimes, we must leave the past behind." He passed his open hands across the upright strands of grass, letting their gentle touch glide against his outstretched palms.

"You would let another woman die a slow, cruel death while you go about your own selfish business on the other side of the world?"

His lips quivered, afraid to say the name. "Je-an was my wife." He paused, wiping at his eye with a finger. "And it's true: I failed in my duty to her. Many times, not just the one. But the girl..."

"Is alone. Helpless. Frightened."

A humorless laugh followed a splash from a nearby wave. "Somehow, I doubt your intentions for either one of us. Just like the poor tanner who never had a chance once you sank your claws into him. No," he ripped a handful of grass from the earth and tossed it into the water, "you're trying to get me killed is what you're doing."

"You're wrong," it answered, equal parts truth and conviction seeping from the being's words. "I have the power of life and death, Arach, and I want you to live. You know I speak the truth."

The words sent a chill up his spine, into his chest, and out in waves through each tense limb. He shivered. "Why?"

"Come with me. I will show you." The grey eyes turned upon the traveler, looking him up and down. "You will do amazing things."

His head and shoulders drooped, the weights of confusion, uncertainty, and failure weighing him down. "I am powerless, wraith. Just a man."

The coldness touched his shoulder and the being hovered into view. "But I am not."

Water splashed and lapped where sea met land, its rhythm carrying Arach from the present to what very well could be.

"Come with me, Arach. Save yourself. Save the girl."

His fear was an anchor in the earth; he closed his eyes and cut the cord that dragged him further down. "You cannot save me, wraith." The traveler stood, setting his sights on the pier ahead. "You do not have that power. It's time for me to go, to leave this place behind. I've done what I can for the girl."

Anger and seething hatred flowed from the apparition as it followed in the wake of the departing man. "Arach, stay a moment! Let us talk and reason!" it hissed, losing ground with the Arach's every step. Reminders of past mistakes, failures, and countless missteps it hurled the traveler's way, promises of a better life on this side of the sea.

But he ignored the wraith, its frantic words no more than twisted inversions of partial truths. He watched in awe as traveler after traveler passed unperturbed and unconcerned with the sight of the terrible apparition, wondered if it was visible to only him. His hand speared the coins within his pocket, the long, untrembling fingers grasping the silver necessary. His spirits lifted, a man ready to be a traveler no longer, and exchanged the few coins for a one-way ticket home. The polite farewell from a hunch-backed toll keeper went unreturned, and Arach heard nothing but the furious beating of his heart and the incessant, empty pleas of the wild trailing wraith.

The bell resounded and he ran the rest of the way. The long pier suspended above the green translucent sea never faltered, never shifted side to side, and he followed the extension to its furthest extent. Arach leapt across the narrow chasm, felt the ferry lurch from side to side as waves rocked the transport back and forth, a baby safe in mother's arms. Inside the boat, travelers huddled in groups, their heads bowed low in deep discussion, anxiety, or amusement. He breathed in the purity, letting it fill his lungs. He knew he was alone.

Arach turned back to the pier and faced the wraith that hovered in its center. The wide southern gate of the deplorable town was a perfect frame around the accursed haunting shade. "Not coming, then?" The traveler looked west beyond the darkened shadow, giving the stream a final glance. He lifted the canteen at his hip to dry and thirsty lips, tasted its sweetness, and rejoiced in the only souvenir he'd removed from the island.

The ferry pushed off at last, its weight pulled forward by its master the sea. Voiceless, the wraith stared, its dull grey eyes diminishing within the void as each wave pulled the boat ever forward.

One chasm widened as the other one shrunk. He turned his back upon the darkness and set his sights for home.

Afterword

The concept for *Wraith* couldn't have come at a much worse time. One beautiful summer day – July 1st, 2014, to be exact – I entered through the doorway to my small home office in northern Indiana with my mind firmly affixed upon the current task at hand. I had literally just wrapped up my second book *Triumphator* and was sitting down to begin the first chapter of my next book *Foreign Shores*. Before I had even taken a seat, I saw him. There, right in front of me on the wall, his lonely back was turned toward me. I took a step forward, paused before the work of art, and studied the details. Even though I had been attracted to and chosen the print myself, it was an image I'd virtually ignored for a year and a half. It was an old painting of young Tiro sitting on a tree limb, ominous mountain in the distance, peaceful sea at the foot of the trunk.

Of course, it wasn't really Tiro to the unknown artist who painted him, but as I stood there and looked upon the framed art, a story began to unfold itself within my mind. It was a story of three young siblings: twins Tiro and Tara, and their elder brother Torin (who would eventually become Marik). As I stood there, face a mere foot from the framed ancient painting, I was entranced. It was amazing how quickly the story blossomed across my soul those first few minutes. Before I had so much as moved an inch, the basic outline for the first three books of a new series called *Siblings* struck hard and fast. I left the painting where it hung, alone but not forgotten on the wall, and quickly wrote my thoughts down. I studied the frantically scribbled details, knew I had only scratched the surface of this unforeseen engrossing tale.

Like I said, it couldn't have come at a worse time. Readers had already begun to ask for a concrete release date for *Foreign Shores*, the final book in my successful series on Roman general Pompey the Great. "End of the year," I'd tell them, never admitting to anyone – much less myself – how deep the talons of this new tale had already sunk into my soul. During the Summer of 2014 I would rotate between *Foreign Shores* and the outline for *Siblings,* the strain of dueling projects a creative train wreck for a stay-at-home dad also trying to take care of and homeschool his own two kindergarten-age kids. Eventually I set both projects aside (no, not the kids!), a decision that haunted me for the remainder of 2014.

During the Summer of 2015, I sat in front of my computer screen with the intent to pen a short story loosely based on an event my wife and I experienced in December 2007. They were the most frightening nights of our lives. In the short story, I took some liberties and incorporated a haunting dream sequence set beside a shallow flowing stream in a green but empty land. As I traveled along the stream, an earthquake tore a chasm right beneath my feet. It left me alone and confused, separated from my wife still abandoned in the waking world where an unknown presence haunted her. It was a good story: half truth, half fiction, completely frightening. I wanted to make the hair stand up on people's heads, wanted to terrify them as my wife and I were terrified those cold sleepless nights.

I still remember sitting there in front of my

computer screen once it was complete. I was happy and very satisfied as I held my finger above the Post button, excited to share my work with the world. Instead, I fell back in my chair, studied each carefully-penned word once more. I hit Delete, erased the whole thing without a second thought. I realized I cared too much about that lonely man to give him such a small stage supported by a mere 1500 words. I renamed him *Arach,* the Greek word for traveler, wayfarer, exile.

Thus began the journey of *Wraith,* the first chapter of a tale that will likely span a minimum of six books. For my faithful fans with your heads and hearts still turned toward ancient Rome, I give you my apologies. *Foreign Shores* is still a work in progress I hope to have complete in 2016. Look for a collection of short stories set within the same era to be released shortly after this book's publication. I haven't forgotten about you!

Special thanks go out to my small and incredible family. From my amazing wife and kids; to my faithful parents, siblings, and grandparents; all the way to my gracious Texas Rangers-loving Aunt Peggy, with everyone else in between: you are all irreplaceable. Summer 2014 - Summer 2015 was a rough creative patch for me. Thanks for helping me across the chasm to the other, greener side.

So many other friends and family have been invaluable over these last two years. Thanks to all who have stuck around so faithfully through it all: many of you before my first book *Rising Sun* was even halfway complete! Words will never express how special your devotion and loyalty are to me. You each hold a very sacred space within my heart.

Thanks again to Beth Hercules for being such a great professional partner through this career I love so much. Your skill as an editor makes you a vital part of my success; your heartfelt encouragement a welcome addition at the end of some long days spent writing, correcting, and re-writing.

To my old friend Asher Eggleston and my newer friend Jo Gilbert: you two blow my mind each time I see your amazing works of art! Thank you so much for the time you've invested and for understanding the vision I hold within my head and heart. You are both such incredible gifts to the world we live in.

Last but not least, a special thanks to YOU for taking the time to share a journey with me. I hope you've enjoyed it thus far, but we have a long, difficult path ahead. You can expect to find *Slaves,* the next book in our series, in the first part of 2016. Follow along on Facebook for updates, send me your thoughts, and make sure to tell your friends about *Wraith* and all that's yet to come!

CPSIA information can be obtained at www.ICGtesting.com
Printed in the USA
LVOW07s1622130116

470477LV00018B/871/P